# The Ghost in Me

# Acknowledgements

Sincere thanks and gratitude are expressed to my family and to early and final readers of this manuscript—Becca Barlow, Sara Olds, Judy Torres, Alane Ferguson, Lori Nawyn, C Zebleckes, and Rick Walton—your encouragement kept me moving forward.

# The Ghost in Me

## Shaunda Kennedy Wenger

First paperback edition, December 2010
Essemkay Company Productions

This is a work of fiction. All cockroaches, names,
characters, places, organizations, and events
portrayed in this book are products of the author's
imagination. Any resemblance to any organization,
event, actual person, or bug, living or dead, is
unintentional.

...Visit the author at
www.shaundawenger.blogspot.com ...

~ For Nia and her ghostly chair,
and for Joanna, Nathan, and Eric,
because they believed ~

Life is a daring adventure, if nothing at all.

—Helen Keller

 Chapter 1

A cockroach can live for eight days with its head cut off.

At least, that's what Duey Williams is saying—or rather, yelling—right into Cam Anree's ear. They're messing around at the front of the bus, acting like seventh-graders—which we no longer are—and blocking kids from getting on with this eight-days-business.

Well. At least if my mother asks what I learned at school today, I'll have something to tell her. That is, if I were interested in telling my mother anything, which I'm not. Especially anything related to him.

Him, being Duey Williams. For one thing, I don't like him.

This, I can honestly say is true, because I make every effort not to.

Yep, as far as I'm concerned, he can take a big dose of ugly. And it'd make my world a whole lot easier if he did. He's way too cute for my own good. I mean, everyone knows you can't crush on your best friend's boyfriend, right? Even if he is an EX? And even if they *are* back to being friends the way EXes try to be?

The whole situation could end up in nothing but a big bowl of awkward.

Generally, I like to avoid awkward. It makes a good rule.

Actually, it's a new rule, thanks to my mother, who needs to get a grip on acceptable dating behavior. Last I checked, dating your daughter's science teacher wasn't part of it.

I'm serious.

When Wolford Academy held parent-teacher conferences last week, half-way through mine, Mr. Diggs and my mother actually started flirting with each other.

That's right. Flirting. My mother with Mr. Black-rimmed Glasses, Blue Collared Shirts, and Two-inch Sideburns that are Brown Thick and Curly....

Yea-ah.

Basically, I wanted to die.

They wanted a date.

Which meant, I wanted to die again... and become something like Wren.

You see, Wren's already dead, but in a good way.

That's because Wren is a ghost.

That's right, a ghost.

She lives with us. Or, maybe I should say, *we live with her*, because she came with the house. Basically, she and I have grown up together.

Or rather, *I've* grown up all of the fourteen years that I've known her, while Wren, on the other hand, has not. She has been and always will be two months past twelve, for whom the rules of life no longer apply—a down-right luxury in my opinion. Wren gets to come and go wherever, whenever, she pleases.

But me? I get to stay stuck with the worst situation on earth—with a mother dating Diggs, unless I can come up with a brilliant plan that will keep Mr. Diggs from ever wanting to see my mother again…. Not such an easy task when I'm constantly being distracted by all-things—no-matter-how-disgusting—Duey.

Yes, Duey, an otherwise edible boy with toffee brown hair that gets flipped from his chocolate brown eyes whenever he laughs.

Who can resist toffee and chocolate? Not me. Not anyone. So maybe I shouldn't feel bad about liking the menu.

Roz, my best friend (his EX), is sitting two rows up on the other side of the aisle, getting help on algebra homework from Cass Barnes. Even though she can't see me, I pretend not to notice when Duey pushes past Cam and jumps into the empty seat behind mine.

"Hey, Myri!"

It's hard to ignore a hello like that, so I give him half a nod, half a smile, and turn my head to stare at the gray-speckled grime on the window, while trying to focus on the one, last-remaining, menu-burning reason I have for not paying attention to anything else Duey might want to say.

 I, Myri Anna Monaco, don't like—*can't stand*—bugs.

Chapter 2

"Eight days!" Roz blurts, while rubbing a nine of clubs on her chin. "Can you believe that?"

We're sitting on the floor of my room playing rummy, and at first, having been completely successful in my Ignore-and-Forget-All-Things-Related-to-Duey plan, I have no idea what she's talking about.

"You remember," Roz prods. "The bus? Two days ago? Duey?"

Oh.

*Ew.*

"The bug thing?"

"Yes, the bug thing!" Roz says, rocking from her knees to her toes.

"Completely disgusting." I watch her pick up a red queen and throw down a seven. "Hide your cards, why don't you?"

For people like me, who try hard not to cheat, Roz always makes playing a simple game of rummy down-right frustrating. If she wasn't my best friend, I might be tempted to take better advantage of it.

Well, in a way, I guess I am. There's no way I'm throwing down either of the twos I'm holding. At least, not yet.

Roz smirks and rearranges the cards in her hand, flashing me a Jack of diamonds and two of clubs in the process. I sigh and give my head a shake. Outside of a soccer game, Roz never really plays by the rules. She's more of a take-it-as-it-goes-sort-of-girl, who's never put up a stink about anything.

Anything, that is, except losing Duey.

And her name. It's Rosetta Victoria Lavender Lynnwood. She's already tried to get it legally changed to the one I made up—Roz. But without her parents' approval, she can't. I don't know what they have against a simple name like Roz, but they're making her stick with the twelve syllables they gave her until she's eighteen.

"Let's go," I say, giving Wren a snap.

Yes, I said that to Wren. *The ghost.*

She's playing cards with us, and it's her turn. I've already drawn her a card, and now she needs to get rid of one she doesn't want—something we've been waiting on for thirty seconds now....

Make that thirty-five, because she's taken time to shoot me a hollow, irritated gaze before tapping the third card from the left. Her cards are in a free-standing card tree that Mom usually uses for holiday photos and letters and stuff, but it also serves as Wren's hands for our game, since she can't hold anything.

"Eight days for what?" she asks, her voice clipped with a strong Irish accent.

I pluck the unwanted seven of spades from the tree and toss it on the pile.

"Nothing," I say, flipping a hand at Roz to keep quiet. Wren can be a pest when she wants to get involved where she doesn't belong, which for a ghost, *and a younger ghost at that*, goes for just about everything.

It's a known fact—at least among the few people that know her…. *Wren is a trouble-making pest.*

That's why she's in my room with us—because Mom told me to keep her entertained. With her new clients coming, she couldn't risk Wren getting all weepy and feeling like they needed a hug.

We learned *that* early on. *Don't let Wren hug the guests.* After all, that's how Roz started being able to see her, hear her—from a hug over a scraped knee when she was three—which as Roz grew older, wiser, turned out to be no big deal. Roz likes Wren—at least as much as anyone can like someone who's dead.

But as for the rest of civilization, or in particular, Mom's clients?

Well, they're pretty much in the midst of experiencing death firsthand. And the last thing they want to see when they've come to see Mom about burying their beloved dead, is a ghost. Not even a harmless one like Wren.

"Ya, right. C'mon, now, Myri," Wren says, giving me a squinty look. She isn't a mind-reader, but she knows when I'm not telling the truth.

She also knows when I'm not going to budge. "All right then, Roz. Y' tell me." Wren shifts closer in Roz's direction. "Y' look ripe enough to bounce out of your skin or something. Eight days for what?"

Roz pushes her dark brown hair back over her shoulder and tips her freckled nose in the air. "Even if Myri would let me tell you," she teases, "I don't think you could handle it. It's a bit more than G-rated material."

"G-rated material! How old would y' be thinking I am?" Wren sinks her hands into her hips, where they disappear into the folds of a nightgown that is as gray and washed out as the mist that clings to Ardenport's shores. "I've got more than three hundred years on this blessed earth, and maybe a day or two more."

Roz's eyes flash wide, and are quick to dance with laughter.

"Now, don't ye dare set in on me wretched looks!" Wren says, flying to her feet and pointing a pale finger between us. "I can see it on both your faces, ye'll be wanting to try, but I'm in no mood for it today."

Roz stifles a laugh, as Wren brushes at her skirt. Wren is sensitive about her looks, and I guess she has every right. It's not like there's a ghost mall she can hit up—a sad reality of the spirit world that has left Wren perpetually fashion-challenged. She's been stuck with the same natty hair, the same boxy nightgown, the same laced boots, and the same wool stockings with a patch at the knee ever since the night she died. Which, like she says, was over three hundred years ago when she went out in search of her Molly cow that'd gone missing, only to end up lost, herself, in an early-winter storm.

Wren died of hypothermia, pretty much on the spot where I live now. The land has changed, but Wren's connection to it hasn't. Gram says that's because she has unfinished business.

Gram knows these things. She's a spiritual consultant—kind of like a psychologist, only her clients hover on the couch, instead of lie directly on it. She's never discovered what needs to be done for Wren, though. Although lately, I've been feeling more and more motivated to try, since Wren is becoming more and more like an irritating, younger sister. In real life, that'd be bad enough....

But I guess this is real life, and Wren is as close to a younger sister as I'm ever going to get, only worse, because I don't have any control over her.

The situation is a bit ironic, actually. I'd rather stay faded in the shadows, while Wren would prefer to blaze ahead like a blinding light.

"Okay, okay, I won't be teasing ye," Roz says, giving Wren a wave of her hand.

"And don't be teasing me 'bout how I talk, neither," she replies. "Or, I'll be finding a way to walk in yer walls tonight. Scare yer socks off, I will."

9

Roz half-laughs, shoots me a wink before setting her eyes back on Wren. "Oh, right. Walk through my walls? Ye-ah. Not so scary. But walk through me? Hmm-mmmmaybe a little bit more."

I can't help but nod, while showing the slightest of grins, because she's right. I let Wren do that to me once.

*Once.*

And once was enough. Only she didn't walk through me, she sat—literally—right in my lap, because I'd asked her to.

I thought it was a good idea at the time, but learned in matter of seconds that eating my peas was better than feeling crowded and squashed by a ghost. Plus, I could still taste the peas. And Wren, who had forgotten how much she disliked them, created an unfortunate conflict-of-interest when it came time to swallow.

Mom was startled, to say the least, when Wren popped out of me along with the peas; and she immediately dove into a lecture about the dangers of that kind of sharing, like getting lost, or getting stuck, or getting our brains all turned to mush.

That's what she said. Turned to mush....Which just goes to show she doesn't know what she's talking about. Technically, Wren doesn't have a brain.

"C'mon, Roz!" Wren pleads. "Just tell me!"

"All right. Fine," Roz says, fighting off my attempt to cover her mouth. "Word on the bus is— *Ow!*

"That it—*Ow!*

"Takes eight days for a cockroach to die—*Erg!*—after its head is cut off. *Would you stop?*" Roz stops me from swatting her a fourth time, as Wren jerks back in surprise.

"Ew. That's a tizzy, now, ain't it?"

"Yeah, it's a tizzy, all right," Roz says, pulling her mouth up in a grin.

"Who came up with that?"

"Duey Williams." I can't help it, but saying his name makes my face flush. I squirm, pick up a card, hope Roz doesn't notice.

I don't think she does. She's still smiling, her eyes without focus.

"Is he a devil's child, or something?"

"No," Roz replies, with a hint of pride in her voice. "He's just one of the more well-informed eighth-graders at Wolford Academy."

This comment makes my eyes roll. Roz really needs to work harder at being an EX.

"But how does he know?" Wren asks, more interested in warped facts about the natural world, than the warped perceptions of Roz's mixed-up mind.

"He doesn't," I say, tossing an eight of diamonds on the pile.

Wren scrunches her mouth up tight. "Well, worms can live without their heads, or bods. They'll even grow new ones. And snakes, maybe. And chickens, for a minute or two."

Her eyes grow distant. "I always hated cutting and plucking them chickens. Their rumps always seemed to want to land on me boots—or me toes, if I wasn't wearing any. But roaches are horrible creatures. If anything can live longer, just to spite death—just to make themselves even more miserable, then I believe roaches could do it. I hate roaches. More than chickens."

Roz tips her head. "See, Myri. Wren believes it."

"Yeah, so?"

"So, what do you say?"

"What do I say to what?"

"What do you say to finding out whether it's true or not?"

"Why would I want to do that?"

"For the science fair."

I look at her like she's nuts, which she is, obviously. "Why are we talking about the science fair? I don't even want to do the science fair. For one thing, it's a complete health risk."

"Health risk?" It's Roz's turn to pull a face.

"Yeah. Health risk. You know how I get. Hives. Dry mouth. Shortness of breath. Talking in front of people totally freaks me out."

Roz laughs. "Who said anything about talking in front of people? You can hide behind a poster that explains everything for you. Besides, you don't get that bad."

I scrunch my lips. I hadn't thought of posters.

"Plus, a lot of good could come out of it."

"Good? Good, as in what?"

"For starters, good as in grades. You can't deny yours needs a bit of help. An-nnnd Diggs said everyone has to do something for the fair, no matter what. So you might as well do something that will liven things up. You're always good for that, you know."

I shake my head as if this is the most ridiculous thing I've heard, which it is. "Yeah, right. I'm going to cut heads off bugs for the science fair. *Because it will be fun.*" I laugh, feeling not at all serious. "*That's a great project.*"

"But that's the thing! It *is* a great project!" Roz bounces up to the balls of her toes, squats in front of me, grabs my shoulders for balance. "Look, Myri, no one else will be doing it, which will make it unique. That'll be a bonus in the grade department. At the same time though, it might lower someone's opinion of you." She bores her eyes into mine. "Someone who's dating your mother."

Roz knows about Diggs. "It might be enough to shake him off, don't you think?"

Maybe.

"It won't be that hard. All you have to do is set it up like a normal experiment, follow a few simple steps, record a bit of data—"

"—tend to headless, disgusting bugs," I cut in, trying not to slump under her weight. "No, Roz, I don't think so."

I shake her off and throw down a two of hearts, hoping to divert her attention toward winning a game for once. Sure, I'm skipping turns, but I'm

13

getting desperate. This whole conversation is getting off track.

Plus, I'm actually starting to think she might be right, but for another reason. While Diggs might be put off by it—which could be useful toward relationship sabotage—Duey might like it.

"C'mon," she urges, not giving my sacrificed card a glance. "What's the big deal?"

"About cutting up roaches? Everything. But if you don't think so, you try it. It sounds like it's right up your alley."

On this, I'm dead serious. As far as I'm concerned, Roz and I are living proof of *In Utero* soul-switching. Meaning somehow, someway, our itty-bitty baby selves switched souls before we were born. Because nothing else explains it—why we look like we fit into our families in the physical sense—me with the blonde and dark-eyed Monacos, her with the russet-haired, freckle-faced Lynnwoods—but in the emotional and mental sense, we're always looking into each other's backyard.

Or, in Roz's case, into my mother's lab. Mom preps bodies at the back of the house. She's a mortician. And her funeral parlor—the place where people gather before burial—is the first thing you see when you walk through the front door.

Roz thinks this whole set-up is cool, which is why I'm surprised *she* isn't doing the bug project.

"Well, I would, if I could—" she says, answering my challenge, "—being that it's such a great idea and all, but I can't. My project is done."

"Already?" The science fair is three weeks away.

"Yep. I grew germs from swab samples I collected around school. I even collected some from Mr. Slayer's toilet seat."

"Tell me you didn't."

"Did," Roz says, before breaking into a laugh. "Wren helped me. She told me when the coast was clear."

"You were at school? Helping Roz?" That's a first.

Wren nods, looking for my approval.

"And I'll help with yers, too," she says. "I was always good with a knife."

"You can't hold a knife," I say, feeling irritated.

"And get this," Roz says, waving her hands through Wren's, as she holds them up for a pitying look. "*His* was the dirtiest place!"

"Mr. Slayer's?"

"Yep. C'mon, I'll show you!"

"You can wait. Believe me, you can wait," I say.

But I know where we'll be heading next. Because if Roz is right, I'm going to want to see if Mr. Slayer, grand principal of Wolford Academy, part-time preacher at the pulpit, *really will* have a lot of explaining to do about the secret lives in his toilet.

## Chapter 3

As it turned out, Duey wasn't making things up.

There were all sorts of universities studying this cockroach phenomenon and posting their findings online, which was good. Because it meant I didn't need to catch roaches on my own to get the project done. Labs actually sold them.

The bad thing was, I had to buy them in bulk; and the smallest box held one hundred.

One hundred!

Ye-eah.

Let me just say, working with that many roaches was no easy task. I mean, have you ever held a cockroach?

I hadn't. And I learned right away it required *a really good grip*, as in, squeeze them between your thumb and your forefinger, so they can't get away (one did). Ignore the touch of their little brown legs wrapping around your knuckle, doing their best to cling tight, while their head—their poor, pointy head—swivels from side to side, steered by skinny antennae....

It was gross. Completely and totally gross.

But still, I got busy. I had to. My life—and all its secret intentions—was hinged on this project.

Needless to say, it was met with mixed reviews on Science Day. Love it or hate it, all of Wolford Academy was drawn to it, repeatedly, with a resounding and unending chorus of *Ewwws!* and *Awesomes!* and *Coo-ooools!*

One-by-one and two-by-two, students would press their noses up to the tank, look at the bugs that still crawled inside, and ask me questions—which I mostly ignored.

After all, I had a big poster that worked well for explaining the project without me. So well, that aside from the time Diggs came by, I stood behind it for nearly the entire fair, just like Roz suggested.

But *nearly* is where I went wrong. *Nearly* is what happens when events occur that you don't plan for. *Nearly* is what gets you in trouble when kids don't move on, even when they're given a summary card that answers their questions.

*Nearly* was Kate Humphreys, who tried taking my experiment to a whole new level with a flashlight by shining it in the tank, saying, "Walk toward the light! Walk toward the light!" *Nearly* was Kent Larsen, who kept sticking front ends of the living, but headless, bugs together. Two bugs got stuck that way, and I found out that unsticking them made them gooey, kind of like what happens when peeling a scab.

But the worst offender—the whole reason everything went wrong—was Brittley Weatherfield, Wolford Academy's finest when it comes to the dramatic arts.

Seriously. The girl has gotten the lead role in every Wolford play since third grade. Not only does she have an agent and a website, she's been invited to a handful of casting calls for Disney—not that she's gotten any parts, and not that it matters. The point is, the girl was born to live a life-blown-out-of-proportion, which didn't work well for me when she blew that life into mine.

And she did it without even looking at my project.

She was checking out Roz's (rather squeamishly), when two little girls came up to see my bugs. They couldn't have been more than six years old, *and what they were doing at our science fair in the middle of a school day, I'll never know*, but apparently, someone thought it would be a good place for a cute set of pony-tailed twins to learn something.

Well. These girls were either severely deprived in the pet department, or felt inclined to adopt everything with legs (but not necessarily heads). They kept asking if they could take my bugs home.

That's right, *home*.

They begged, all the while trying to show what nice cockroach parents they'd be by petting them.

I should have known that wasn't a great idea. But I figured, *Hey, if these girls want to pet headless bugs, I'll let them pet headless bugs.* But then, one of the bugs that the twins was holding died in her hand. *And even though 80-plus carcasses were pinned to a poster, showing what had happened many times before*, those girls got way over-excited and acted like they'd never seen anything like it.

Their arms started flailing, their mouths started yelling, their feet started stamping, and before I knew what was happening, that bug got tossed in the air.

It landed in Brittley Weatherfield's hair.

When Brittley saw that bug hanging by its leg, swinging back and forth in front of her face—bumping her nose, her lip, her cheek, because it was all tangled up, and getting even more tangled with all her jumping around—not only did she scream, she convulsed. And spun. And wiggled her tongue in and out of her mouth.

I would have thought that after a few good moments of this, she would have calmed down. Reclaimed her dignity. But she didn't. She went on screaming until she fell on the table holding Eddie Lightning's volcano.

As luck would have it, that fall tipped the table up and launched Eddie's volcano into the air, where it exploded all over Vice Principal Haydens. And me, who tried to save him.

Yes, I did.

Much to the surprise of everyone, including myself, I moved in to save the vice principal of Wolford Academy. Tackled him like a defensive-end for the New York Giants.

But, as Wren would say, it was all for naught.

Despite my heroic attempt at diverting disaster, Haydens took it upon himself to deliver a note from Slayer later that day.

*Please meet me in my office tomorrow at 8 am-sharp.*

And here I am.

Since school starts at nine, and Slayer is allowing a full hour for the meeting, I figure I'm in deep doo-doo, and like my roaches, will soon be flailing—struggling to survive without a head.

## Chapter 4

"He's a chairful of man, ain't he?"

"Shhhh—!"

—Now that was dumb. It's not like Slayer can see Wren's face poking through the painting of George Washington on the far wall.

I whip my attention back to him and press back against the cold, gray metal of my chair. Slayer tips his polished head from side to side, cracking the vertebrae in his neck.

"Something wrong, Miss Monaco?" His eyes flicker with quiet restraint, making my stomach quiver. He leans forward into the edge of his enormous mahogany desk, waiting for an answer.

"No, just a sneeze. Sorry." I rub my nose with my finger, pointing at the window, hoping Wren will take the hint and go.

Instead, she moves from the painting to hover under the light in the center of the room. The glare from Slayer's head weakens in her shadow, and he glances distractedly at the window to his right before opening the manila file lying in front of him.

Giving a tsk, Wren dips down and spins through it, nearly sending me out of my chair to grab her. Not that I could.

"Remember, Myr, there's nothing so bad, that it couldn't be worse!" This is what she tells me before pinching herself out.

That's what I call it when she disappears. *Pinching*.

I give a quick check under my chair, behind the door, to make sure she's gone.

"Are you sure nothing's wrong, Miss Monaco?" Slayer sets the larger of his steely gray eyes on me. The other, being prone to wander, gazes unnervingly at something past my shoulder.

"Uh, no, nothing." I make my fingers ease their grip on my seat, wishing I could take a quick look through the halls to make sure Wren isn't out there.

"Good. Let's get on with it, shall we?" He pats the papers in front of him.

I wince, swallow. "Look—Mr. Slayer, about the project, I'm sorry it got a little crazy, but you see, it really wasn't my own idea. There are all sorts of universities—"

Mr. Slayer waves me off. "Yes, yes, the project. Rather creative, Myri." He pauses, takes in a breath, lets it out. "A bit unlike anything Wolford has ever seen. Yet, despite all the good things that teacher of yours, *Diggs*, had to say, *if you ask me—*"

"Wait. Diggs liked it?"

"*Mister* Diggs," he says, correcting me. "According to the records in the computer, he gave you an A."

"*An A?*"

Crap! My whole plan was a flop then. I'd wanted a good grade, but not *that good*. My mom will be so happy. With me. With him.

"Yes, an A," he says, obviously not pleased.

And neither am I.

I wasn't aiming to be a star student. Far from it. Basically, I wanted Diggs to believe I was downright demented, but in a B or B-minus sort of way. I could've lived with that.

Slayer clears his throat. "As I was saying, I found the basic idea of the project rather lacking in regards to real science—science that actually gets us somewhere... somewhere, shall we say, spinning atop new horizons, burning with questions, both meaningful and profound...." Slayer waves his hand up, focusing on nothing in particular (thank God) on the ceiling.

Finally, he brings his hand down, rubs the dark armrest of his chair. "Do you understand what I'm saying?"

I shake my head.

He tips his. "Well, maybe it doesn't really matter. When put in a broader context, what does matter, is the creativity of the project; because that is the *very crux* of our meeting today. Specifically, taking opportunities to use that creativity of yours in a productive outlet."

He leans forward, curling the corner of a blue sheet of paper between his thumb and forefinger. "After review of your file, Myri, I don't see that you're involved in any ECSAs."

"ECSAs?"

"Yes."

It takes a moment for those letters to sink in.

*Oh.*

I give him a questioning look, as if I don't know what he's talking about.

"Extra-curricular school activities," he says flatly. "You've missed out on them for nearly the first half the trimester, which is a tremendous oversight on the administration's part."

I squirm in my chair. "This isn't about the science fair?" I ask, suddenly wishing it was.

"No, although, I have to say, if it wasn't for the science fair, I might never have looked at your file."

Great. Now would be a good time *for me* to disappear.

Slayer taps his pencil on its eraser once, twice, swivels in his chair. "But not to worry, Miss Monaco. I've forgiven the situation. And I've taken steps to correct it."

"You have?"

"Yes, with what I think will turn out to be the *perfect solution.*"

Chapter 5

Roz, Queen-of-Subtle, is waiting by the office door, with Elise Fowler and Cass Barnes when I walk out. Between the three of them, I know that everyone in eighth grade has heard where I spent the morning.

"Did you get detention?"

Pushing Roz's shoulder with mine, I steer her down the hall. "Funny question coming from a girl who told me everything would be all right to begin with."

Elise jogs to catch up. "But that was before you doused Haydens with sticky lava."

"And before you cut up one hundred roaches," Cass adds, peering at me over Roz's shoulder.

"Eighty-nine, actually. I only cut up 89. Didn't you read my summary card?" I'm joking, but still. A girl has to defend herself. "Ten bugs were left alone to show how they would've lived, if they'd never been touched."

"Uh, that only adds up to ninety-nine," Cass says, doing the math in her head. "Didn't you order one hundred?"

"Well, yeah, but one got away. *Don't* tell my mother."

Cass and Elise snicker and say they're telling, as I check Roz's watch. We only have a few minutes before class, and as usual, the eighth-grade hall is crammed with kids. There's no clear path to my locker.

"So, did you?" Roz tries again, hoisting her backpack on her shoulder, swiveling with me through the crowd to keep up.

"Did I what?" A few girls glance in my direction and laugh.

"*Did you get detention?*" Roz pulls me into her, as I'm about to skirt away.

"Ye-ahhh," I gush, after regaining my balance. "I mean, no. I'll tell you what happened in a sec." Wriggling from her grip, I dodge through the oncoming traffic.

With a quick spin of the combination, the door opens. Grabbing my books and binder, I shove my coat inside. I'm about to make my way back, when I see I don't need to. Roz is beside me, standing with her arms crossed, along with Cass and Elise.

"Okay, okay, I didn't get detention. I got drama."

Roz pulls a face, takes a step back. "Drama? What do you mean, you got *drama*?

Sick at the thought of it, I hesitate, scuff my heel on the floor.

Roz fans her hands. *"Drama means what,* exactly?"

Cass starts hopping, like we're playing a game. Even though she's bouncing like a bunny, her short, high-lighted hair, slick with gel and spray, doesn't move. "Oh! I know!" she says. "Do you mean drama, as in, wailing, crying, oh-how-could-you-do-this-sort-of-thing-drama?"

I take a quick breath. "Close. But no."

"Drama, as in you-should-be-ashamed-of-yourself-sort-of-drama?" Elise says, wagging her finger, squinting one eye through her gold-rimmed glasses.

"No. Worse. Drama, as in drama club, sort-of-drama."

Roz's face pushes up in confusion. She lets her hands go to her hips.

I let out a huff. "I didn't get detention, Roz. I got *drama club.* Slayer took away my study hall. Now I'm in drama club, for first period, for the rest of the trimester."

"Are you kidding me? What kind of punishment is that?"

"It's not a punishment. But for me, it may as well be. I don't want to do drama. Getting up in front of an audience isn't my thing."

"Why not?" Cass asks, with a giggle. "I mean, you tend to be very dramatic, like yesterday. Plus, I'm in drama. It's fun."

27

Elise throws her head back and laughs. "If I'd known being a delinquent was so easy, Myri, I'd have started walking on your side of the tracks a long time ago, joined forces with roaches, done all kinds of things."

"Yeah, right," I scoff. Elise loves causing trouble. Or at least, thinking up ways to make it. With her, it's the doing-part that never seems to get done.

"Besides," I continue, feeling a need to defend myself. "I wasn't being a delinquent. I was conducting a science experiment."

"Oh, yeah," Elise's eyes wrinkle up. "And you got sentenced for it?"

"No, I got drama, because I never signed up for ECSAs."

I get blank stares in reply.

"Extra-curricular student activities. I never signed up for an academic club at the beginning of the year."

"Oh, those!" Elise's voice fills with understanding and surprise. "You never did that? I thought everyone was supposed to sign up for a club. It's like a requirement, or something. They're kind of like classes."

"I know, but I thought I could get out of doing one if I signed up for study hall."

I don't tell them I knew Duey had signed up for study hall, too.

"So, what was the problem, then?" Roz asks.

"I needed parent-permission."

"Ahhh," Cass says. Elise joins her with a nod. "You didn't get it?"

I shake my head. "As of this morning, the consensus between my mother and the fine people who teach here is I can work on my grades—average as they are—at home."

Roz gives me a nudge. "Why didn't you tell Slayer to put you in art? I'm in art."

"I did, but it's full, which is the reason I didn't sign up to begin with. All the good clubs were taken by the time I got to them. All except debate and drama. Which are still the only choices I have now. So, Slayer chose for me."

I shake my head, let out a breath. "Some choice. I can't even *think* the word drama, let alone say it without getting itchy all over. Look at this." I hold out my arm. "*Welts.* Big red welts. And they're spreading. And I'm not even near a stage."

I try to give myself a hug, settle for grabbing my elbows. "It's crazy. The whole idea of it. I can't act. Can't dance. Can't sing. Can't even get up in front of a class and talk. Ask anyone who wanted to know about the cockroaches yesterday. Or, anyone who's going through the speech segment with me in English right now—.'"

"I'm in English with you now."

Crap.

That's Duey.

And he's right behind me.

Before I can think of an excuse to run away, Roz spins me around. It's amazing what a simple navy blue tee-shirt and jeans can do to a girl when they're combined with a green backpack casually slung over a shoulder and topped off with a mouth turned up in a grin.

"Hey, Myri."

They can send a girl's heart into convulsions.

And to think Roz started it.

"Duey," Roz says, making her voice go serious to draw his attention. "You're just what we need. Tell Myri she's going to be okay."

"Why?"

Squeezing my arms, she hooks her chin on my shoulder. "Myri's been sentenced to drama club."

His mouth drops in mock surprise. "Drama club!" He stumbles back against my locker, as if he's been shot, making it clang and rattle. "For the bug thing?"

Oh, well. At least he knows the project was mine. For future reference. Which almost makes the future pain and suffering I'll face worth it. Because based on how he checked it out at the science fair, I know he liked it.

"Yep." Roz hands me off to Cass, so she can follow him, as he backs down the hall. "And I'd say you owe her one, since this never would have happened, if it weren't for you."

"Me?" Duey looks bewildered. "What did I do?"

"You gave us the roach idea." Stepping forward, she bumps him with her hip, which bangs him into more lockers.

"Ooooft! That hurt."

Yes, like a knife through the heart. Because it's playful moments like this that show he and Roz should still be a couple.

Rolling off the lockers, Duey straightens and wiggles his fingers at me. "Well, Myri, make sure you take Tank with you." He juts his chin down at Roz, who is glowing over her new nickname. "Ardenport Theater is haunted, you know."

"Oh, you're so funny," I say.

"Roz," he says, turning to her, placing a hand over his heart. "I'm honestly trying to look out for your friend's best interest. Tell her I'm being serious."

"Well, thanks," Roz says, pushing him on the arm, "but look at her. Ghosts are the least of her worries. The girl's problems lie with performing for an audience. Besides, Wolford Academy has its own theater, thank you very much."

He gives a crooked smile. "If you say so."

"Yes, we say so," Cass says, linking her arm through mine. She gives him a salute. "So, don't worry, Duey. She'll be protected, wherever we are."

"Good."

"But, just so you know," Cass adds, tipping her ear to her shoulder, "you could be protecting her, too, if you hadn't ducked out on drama this year. Maybe you should join—"

"Mr. Williams!" For once, I'm thankful to hear Slayer's voice. He steps into view at the end of the hall.

Duey stands taller, trying to look innocent.

Slayer circles his hand, beckoning Duey to come toward him. "In my office."

"Now? But I'll be late for class."

Slayer points down the hall behind him. "Yes. Office. *Now*."

Duey sighs and starts forward. After a moment Roz calls out, "Careful! I hear his office is haunted!"

My head jerks at the remark. But I don't have time to give it much thought, nor the giggle from Roz that follows, because a moment later, the bell rings, and everyone scatters like a deck of tossed cards.

Everyone, that is, but me.

I stay where I am—like a scrappy two of clubs pressed flat to the floor. Because compared to where I need to go, the middle of the hallway seems like a much happier place.

And it is. Until Cass jogs back to get me.

Taking my hand, she pulls me along, away from the fifty minutes where I passed the time secretly staring at Duey, toward last place I ever wanted to be.

## Chapter 6

"What's he doing here?"

"Hmmm?" Cass stops next to me in the doorway and looks to the front of the room where Diggs is standing.

"He's not— He can't—" I keep my words steady, my thoughts clear, so I don't say something I'll regret. After all, Diggs is a science teacher. He teaches science, not drama. Which means, he's simply here for a visit. To talk with the drama teacher. Who is…. I look around. "Who's the drama teacher?" Slayer hadn't mentioned it. And I hadn't thought to ask.

"Diggs," Cass replies. "He took over last year after Miss Nanna left."

Oh, no. One class with Diggs was bad enough. But now, two?

My stomach turns sour and twists into knots, as I watch him scoot into a sitting position on top of the teacher's desk. It's empty, so there's plenty of room. He crosses his legs, stretches him arms wide, gives everyone a welcoming smile. "Good morning, class! Good morning!"

*Is this why my mother went along with Slayer's solution?*

"Yes, hello!" he continues, as the last bell rings and the chatter simmers around him. "Find a seat, so we can get started."

I guess that means us.

Cass tips her head toward to a pair of empty desks at the back of the room.

"You didn't tell me," I mutter, scuttling behind her.

"Tell you what?"

"That Diggs does drama."

She shrugs, as she sits down. "I didn't think to."

Which makes sense. She doesn't know about Diggs and my mom. To her, his being here is no big deal. ECSAs *are* led by teachers, after all.

I open my binder, prop it on the desk, peer over its cover. With his arms held out, palms turned up, Diggs doesn't look like a science teacher.

But his tan pants, black-rimmed glasses, and light-blue button-down shirt aren't screaming, "I'm a drama teacher!" either.

Okay, so maybe his style of sitting is. And his tan stocking feet—he's kicked his brown loafers off. And his voice, which I can already tell is a bit more dramatic than the way it sounds in the lab.

Diggs claps his hands. "Let me say it again! Find a seat on your desk! Or, in your *chair*. Whichever you prefer, so long as *you're in a comfortable place* where you can see me."

He gives a satisfied nod.

"Great. Good to hear your voices so early in the day." I follow his eyes, as they move around the room from Cam Anree, who I hadn't noticed on the far side, to Gerica Walters, a stony, pale-faced goth who paints her eye-lids black, and finally to the one person I never wanted to be near again. Brittley. She squares her pink-sweatered shoulders and grins at Londyn Times, a girl sitting next to her in the front row.

Diggs nods, lifts his eyes to the rest of the class. "Today, for our opening exercise, we're continuing with our visualization techniques. But we're going to take it a step further into the *metaphysical*, by tapping into the energy at our core." He touches his chest with a fist. "Because drama, as you all know, is about harnessing energy. And *showing* energy. And *feeling* energy." He lifts his fist high, tightens his fingers more. "Ultimately, it's about sharing energy. With the audience. With each other. With *everyone* in the theater who wants to be swept up into a story as it unfolds."

Diggs must have taken a class from Miss Nanna. She was my health teacher last year, and she talked about this new-age, mumbo-jumbo stuff all the time. I imagine she talked about it here, too.

"*But*," Diggs continues, raising a finger. "Before you can do any of that, before you can show, feel, or share your energy, you have to know where that

35

energy rests. How to harness it. And most importantly, *how to control it*. This will be an important exercise as we prepare for our play, the choice of which I'll go over in a few minutes."

I raise my hand.

"Yes? Is there a question?... Oh, Myri. Hello. Welcome to the club—I'd forgotten. Everyone, this is Myri. She's joining us for the rest of the trimester. Some of you know her, I'm sure."

I hear a snicker at the front of the room, as Brittley turns and gives me a vicious smile. Leaning toward Londyn, she whispers, making Diggs lower his eyebrows and bring a finger to his lips. He returns his attention to me. "I'm sorry, do you have a question?"

"Well, I just... I mean...." I let out a quick breath, hang my mouth open, and somehow, my voice finds a way in. "This exercise doesn't apply to people who'll be working on the set, does it?"

Brittley snickers again.

"An excellent question, Myri, because yes, it does apply to everyone, no matter where they end up working." He hops off the desk, raises his arms, pirouettes in a circle. "Just as a play's performance lives and breathes from its actors, it *also* lives and breathes from its props, its sets, its costumes, its lights."

Pumping his hands up by his sides, he continues, "The audience is going to *feel* the energy from *everything* in the show. So, yes, it applies to you,

Myri, and to everyone in this room—whether they're using a hammer, a needle, or a brush.

"And I'll also say this. *Our show is going be tied to the energy that we have right here, right now,* from this exercise we are about to begin, to the first line uttered at rehearsal, to the final moment when the curtain draws to a close."

Diggs reaches back and pulls himself onto the desk again. He holds his hands out in front of him. "So. Are we ready to harness? To feel? To share?"

Half of the class wobble their heads from side-to-side. Others exchange glances of amusement. A few tap their chests like Diggs. Some, like Brittley, wiggle their fingers. And at least one—Cam, in particular—shakes his hands from his wrists, as if getting ready for a heavy-weight fight.

Cass crosses her legs on her seat next to me and turns her focus on Diggs; I, however, stay as I am, sitting like a normal person—feet on floor, hands on desk, butt in chair.

"Now, I'd like you to hold your hands in front of you, like you're holding a tennis ball," he says. "Keep your palms facing each other, but don't let your hands touch."

He waits for the class to copy his movements.

They do.

After a moment, I do, too.

"Good, now close your eyes. You should begin to feel a warmth sitting between your palms." He pauses.

"Once you feel that heat, focus on it. See if you can feel a pulse, the flow of energy as it warms up and moves from one palm to the other....

"Do you all feel that?"

I do, actually.

"That, folks, is an energy ball. Now, while your eyes are closed, rotate your hands around it, focus on whatever color comes to mind. Whatever color your *mind's-eye* sees."

Color?

Okay. Whatever.

...Red. I think I see red. And white.

Red, with little flashes of white.

"Good, once the energy feels steady, let's see how far apart you can move your hands. But do it slowly. I don't want you losing *that heat*—that connection to your internal energy."

The heat dips, but it doesn't take long for a stronger warmth to return, which is pretty cool, because it actually feels like I'm holding something, even though I'm not.

I sneak a peek at Diggs to make sure I know what he's talking about, then take a quick look around. A few kids are trying the rotation thing. Samantha McQue, a girl I don't know very well, and who is sitting on the other side of Cass, is pumping her hands in and out, like she's playing a set a bag pipes.

Cass snorts at her, juts her chin. "Cheater!"

Exactly.

"Quiet, please." Diggs's voice cuts through the room. "Remember, *this is your energy*. The energy that flows inside of *you*, at every minute of the day. And right now, you're literally holding it in the *palm of your hands*...." He pumps his arms. "This is the energy that helps *project* who you are, what you want to *be*, what you *want* the world to see.

"See how far you can tap into it. See how far you can move your hands apart. See how big that energy field can become."

How big it can become? I'm actually getting a bit concerned about that. Because I've been moving my hands further and further apart without really thinking about it and my hands are about as wide as a beach ball.

And even though after each move, the energy dips a little, it always surges right back up—which scares me, because I have no idea what I'm doing.

I peek my eyes open again, and see my arms are as wide as Diggs has his.

"You say I'm a cheater?" Samantha hisses at Cass. "Look at Myri!"

I snap my eyes shut to ignore her. My face flushes with heat.

"Uh, mine's not working," Cam says.

"And what are we supposed to do with these energy balls, anyway?" Brittley asks.

Diggs hums a moment in thought. "How about we see if you can share it with a neighbor? Pass your hands gently through one another's. See how it feels when your energies are combined."

Okay. I don't think that's a good idea, because my energy is getting heavy.

Or, maybe my arms are just getting tired.

My eyes blast open at the touch of a familiar chill on my arm.

Wren.

Not only is she standing next me, she's moving her hands in the space between mine.

"It's pink, Myr! A pinkish reddish pink!"

I have no idea what she's talking about, nor a clue as to why she's acting like what she's doing—dropping in on class—is no big deal.

"And hers is blue," she says, tipping her head at Cass. "A really light blue."

I let out a quiet huff. "Go away," I hiss.

"But I wanted to see what ye'll be doing, Myr. Make sure nothing got worse, before it got better. Looks like yer off to a jolly bit of fun. I might be wanting to give this a try."

Give it a try? My eyes goggle at her. What is she even doing here?

She holds her hands up like mine.

Out of the corner of my eye, I see Cass shift and give me a look.

Great. I'm not even half-way through my first day in drama and I'm already looking like an idiot. I need to get out of here, or at least get away from Wren.

I stand slowly, as if to copy the kids who are moving out of their seats to share their energies.

Wren smiles wide. "Give it a throw, Myri!" She holds her arms out, as if ready for a game of catch.

But I'm not playing. Instead, I step toward the back of the room, giving her a look that could kill—which doesn't mean much, since she's already dead.

"I'll catch it for y' now! Just like he said!"

No, he didn't say that.

"Stay away," I mouth, which I know doesn't look good to anyone who may be watching. I roll my shoulders and twist them from side to side to make it look like I'm stretching.

"But I can feel it. And I can see it, too." Wren's face is filled with awe, as she looks from my hands to hers. I wish she'd stop—pinch herself into her own side of the world—but she keeps coming closer, with her eyes spilled over like empty, black saucers, like she's in a trance, and no matter what I say, I'm not going to be heard—at least, not by her.

I back up until I bump the supply cabinets, shake my head—barely—because we, or rather, *I*, definitely have an audience now. No one can see her, when she moves her hands between mine. No one can feel the chill that comes with them.

Without thinking, I turn to give the energy ball a toss; but as I do, I trip and lunge forward. It almost feels like I'm bowling.

Cass breaks into laughter. "Look who says they're not ready for drama."

## Chapter 7

I can see them now.

The words on my gravestone.

*Died from embarrassment.*

And honestly, I'd be happy with that sort of accomplishment.

Really, I would. Not only would it land me in the *Guinness Book of World Records* for being the first person on the planet to be done in by such a thing, my mother might hold Diggs responsible. Causing the death of one's daughter would probably be enough to drive two people apart. Not that it would matter if I wasn't around to enjoy it. But then again, I wouldn't be left listening to Diggs's calls of, "Bravo! Bravo!" either.

It's all I can do to keep myself from crawling back to my seat.

Diggs continues to clap, even though he's the only one. "Well done, Myri! *Well done.* I'd say you *commanded* that performance. Did everyone see that?"

I hope not.

"Well, if you didn't, you missed brilliance in action, people. Brilliance in action." Diggs quickly rubs his hands together. "Because I must say, Myri made excellent use of the space around her, while tapping into her creative abilities to show quite effectively, and *quite uniquely*, another thing that might be done with an energy ball." He looks at me with wonder, addresses me directly. "Bowling? What made you think of it?"

Rather than reply, I slip deeper into my seat, rub my eyes, take a quick glance around to make sure Wren is really gone.

"Although…."

He's still talking?

Diggs splays his hand at the side his mouth. "As a general rule, we probably don't want to let go of our energy like that. It's kind of a good thing to hold on to." He spins to stand at the back of his desk, raps his fingers on top of it. "Nevertheless, that demonstration has given us a wonderful introduction to our next discussion."

Brittley raises her hand. Diggs give her a nod.

"Is that, *How To Make a Fool of Yourself 101?*"

The class erupts again, and Diggs pats his hands in the air. It takes a while until everyone settles down.

"In the future, Miss Weatherfield, let's refrain from such comments. Unless, of course, you're being so gracious as to act the fool yourself?"

Brittley's lips clamp into a firm line.

"I didn't think so. Now, as I was saying, we're ready to move on to the next segment of this class—*or club*, rather. One you've all been waiting for. One we've talked about." He takes in a breath, waves his arms as if encouraging everyone else to do the same, then lets it all out with a bow. "*Auditions.*"

Chapter 8

My heart has continued to pound through second hour, making my mind a blur, making me miss what the entire lesson has been about.

Well, I did catch a little—something about China's Great Wall. But as far as *Why* it was built, and *Who* they were trying to keep out, and exactly *Who* was in charge of the whole deal to begin with?... I have no idea.

To make matters worse, Mr. Scanlin has just announced a quiz for tomorrow, which means Sarah Turner won't be lending me her notes. Not even for a free item from the snack bar at lunch. Which means, if I don't calm down, I'll be carrying fifty pounds of books home by the end of the day—with the first ten being the *Our World* book from under my desk—for all the good it'll do me. Mr. Scanlin is known for quizzing us on material that's not in the text.

"I am so dead," I say to Roz, after pulling her aside in the hall. "There's just no way—."

I shake my hands through my hair, trying to push out the words that are jumbled in my mouth. But it's no use. They're not going to budge. Giving up, I thrust the script at her.

Roz frumps her face at the title. "Beauty and the Yeast?"

I nod, then keeping nodding, knowing she'll connect the dots.

"Is this a typo?"

No. Not those dots.

I shake my head. "No, that's the real name of the play. It's a spin-off, set in a bakery."

Roz gives me a look, as she fans through the script.

Okay, so she's not picking up on the fear streaming through me.

"Everyone has to try out," I blurt to give her a clue. "*Everyone.* Starting tonight. At the town theater, because that's where the play will be done."

"Ardenport Theater? Like Duey said?"

I nod. Duey, apparently, is well-connected.

Roz lets out a breath. "That's fast."

I half-shrug. "Not if you're everyone else. Everyone else has known about it for a couple weeks, but not me, thanks to this morning, thanks to this wonderful thing I call my life."

"Can't you skip out?"

"No. Auditions are mandatory. If I don't go, I fail. *Drama* is actually a *pass/fail course.* Just a *minor detail* Slayer forgot to mention."

"Well, they all are. That's the way ECSAs work. You know that. That's why they're mandatory."

"Study hall is pass/fail?"

It's Roz's turn to nod.

Okay, so maybe I shouldn't be surprised I didn't know this. Study hall doesn't become a choice for Wolford students until they're in eighth grade. And I'm only in eighth grade.

"But it's no big deal," Roz says, finally reading my dread of the situation. "It's not like Diggs expects everyone will give an amazing audition. You'll pass, even if it stinks. Just mumble through it like you would anything else you're not ready for."

I ignore the twinge I feel at the comment, let out a short huff. "But I don't think I'll be able to mumble. I'm totally freaked out. I'm going to be shaking, and stuttering, and looking like an idiot."

"Well, you look like an idiot in English, too," Roz says, bopping me on the arm. "But that doesn't keep you from getting up there and reading your essays, does it?"

I step back, give her an I-don't-believe-you-just-said-that look. Because even though I know I have a problem talking in front of a class, I still have limits on how many ways I can stand to look bad.

"I'm just joking," she says, waving me off. "You do fine in English. I don't know why you don't think so. It's going to be okay. Just take a deep breath and chill. Do what you need to do to relax."

"Relax? This isn't English class, Roz. There won't be a podium for me to hide behind, or lean on when I think I'm going to pass out. I have to be up high. By myself. On a stage. In front of people who were actually born to do this sort of thing."

I wrap my arms around the top of my head, then let them fall to my sides. "What am I going to do?"

Roz shrugs, hands back the script, as she makes a move to get to her next class. "Well, if you think it's going to be that big a deal, then get Wren to do it."

I do a double-take.

That statement was rather matter-of-fact.... I'm not sure I've heard her right.

"Wren?" For a moment I feel dizzy.

"Yeah. Kind of like the way I let her take my history test."

"Sh— She took your test?" Now my head is shaking back and forth uncontrollably. I can't believe it. "How? When?"

Roz nods, gives another shrug, as if what she just said is the most normal thing to say on the planet. "Last week. I just kind of let her fill in for me for a day—or, step into me. For an hour. It's amazing how much she remembered. And the details she put in my essay quest—"

"She took your test? As in, possession? *Bodily possession?*" I try keeping my voice down, but it's hard to do, when my insides are erupting like a geyser.

I pull her over to the lockers—not that it gives us any privacy. Although, actually, after a quick look around I see it's not something I need to worry about. We're the only students left in the hall. "People call in priests to stop that sort of thing," I hiss. "Haven't you seen *The Exorcist?* Just the clips are enough to freak anyone out!"

"That's if you have a *mean* ghost, not one that's nice. Wren is nice. She was helping me."

"Where—" I shake my hands by my ears. "Where were you while this was happening?"

"I told you. I was in history class."

"No, I mean, where were *you*, Roz, the person inside you that makes you, *you*. It's not like you could step out for a cup of tea."

"Oh." Roz frowns. "I wasn't anywhere, I guess. I mean, I was still there—still inside me. I just kind of felt pushed off to the side a bit. But not really. I mean, I could feel myself holding the pencil, and I could still read the questions, but I could hear Wren reading and answering the questions, too. It was sort of weird, but after a few minutes, I got used to it, and then I sort of let go. Soon, she was doing all the work for me."

"And when you were done?"

"When she was done, it was easy. We snapped back to normal."

"Snapped back to normal." I repeat the words, my voice full of disbelief.

The bell rings.

We stay where we are, staring at each other, me in shock, her trying to look like what she just said is all perfectly fine.

"Look," Roz says, letting out a breath. "We'll talk later, okay?" She backs down the hall. "You're getting stressed over nothing, Myr. You can either do the auditions, and not get a part. Or, do the auditions with Wren, and still not get the part. Either way, you still pass. You'll be fine, okay?

"Myr?"

When I don't answer, she shrugs, and takes off down the hall.

Yeah. Okay. Sure. I'll just go to class. Act like *everything's fine*. Like my best friend didn't just tell me that the ghost I've been living with my entire life has found a way to live a double-life, literally, inside my best friend, whenever she feels like it.

Okay, so maybe it was just for a one hour class.

And maybe it wasn't really living, because she was only taking a test. On history. About a subject through which she already lived.

But still. Please. Somebody pinch me. Because I swear, I just woke up to a total nightmare.

Or, maybe I've always been living one.

Chapter 9

Elise drops her sack lunch on the table, stands back a moment to eye up the three of us—me, Cass and Roz—in a way that makes me nervous. I've seen that look before, like when she suggested we turn the school parking lot into a skating rink last year in an effort to create a no-school-day, on account of the fact that teachers would find themselves trapped in their cars upon arriving, unable to get to the doors without a pair of ice skates. Fortunately, or unfortunately—whatever the case may be—we never made it past the planning stage.

"Okay, so I've been thinking," she says with a tone of determination.

I poke my fork through my pickle, wave it expectantly.

"And this is the deal," she says. "We're going to make the best of a bad situation."

"Bad situation?" Roz raises her eyebrows, as Elise straddles the stool next to her and sits down. "Which situation would that be? The one where I'm still dumped by Duey. Or, the one where Myri's been dumped into drama club. Or,...?" She points a finger across that table at Cass. "Do you have a bad situation you've not shared with us, yet?"

Cass opens her mouth, tips her head in thought. "My fish hasn't learned how to talk?"

Elise doesn't flinch, even though the three of us laugh. She's all serious, wagging her finger, *specifically*, I notice, at me and Cass. "No, none of that. The Brittley situation," she says. "We're going to fix it."

"Brittley situation?" Cass giggles some more. "I didn't know there was one."

"Yeah, there is. If you're me, there is. And you're going to help me. Either you, or Myri. Whoever comes first. One of you is going to knock her out of the play."

I half-laugh. "That's a joke, right? I mean, this is me, here. How would you expect me to do that?"

Elise gives a quick nod. "By beating her in auditions."

Cass lets out a short huff, taps a hand from her shoulder to mine. "Uh, good thinking, *but again*, look at who you're dealing with."

"I mean it!" Elise replies, her voice rising a notch. She leans forward on her elbows, splays her hands on the table. "If I have to put up with her the way she was last year when I was taking pictures for yearbook, I'm seriously going to hurt someone...."

Elise holds up a hand, telling us to wait while she takes a sip of juice. "You should have seen her," she says, when she finishes. "She kept saying, 'Did you

52

get me? Did you get me?'" Elise struggles with another sip. "I spent most of my time looking for a reason *to miss her*, but somehow she managed to get in every shot. I guess it's hard to avoid getting photos of the lead."

"Maybe we'll get lucky and someone else will get the lead," Cass offers. "But don't count on it being me. When it comes to winning roles, my chances are slim. Last year, I was cast as a tree. You know that."

"But you were a good tree," Roz says, giving her a wink before biting into her sandwich.

"Yeah, I was," she answers wistfully. "The *best* Wolford has ever seen. *And*, I was in the yearbook, thanks to Elise, even if I did blend in too well with the scenery."

Elise nods, drums her fingers while she studies me, looks at Cass, then studies me some more.

I rub my neck, pretending to ignore her, then pull my tray back from the center of the table to spoon up vanilla pudding.

"Myr," she says, waiting for me to look up. Finally, after a long moment of silence, I do. "Myr, you're my only hope. As the newbie, you could be the dark horse in this undertaking."

I raise my eyebrows, fill my mouth with more pudding, and more pudding, as if I could stuff it all the way back to my ears to keep myself from hearing her.

Elise turns a hand, lets out a sigh. "Okay, so maybe beating Brittley to the lead is a stretch, I'll admit. But listen," she begs, "maybe we can do something else." Reaching forward, she grabs my hand to stop me from scraping the thin white lines left on my tray, turns to look at Cass. "If you guys get roles in the play this year, I'll make sure *you're* the ones that get put in the drama spread."

"Even if I'm a tree?" Cass says.

"Even better if you're a tree, because this time I'll put you in the foreground, make sure you upstage whatever character Brittley gets to be."

I shake my head, as Cass giggles and knocks fists with Elise. Roz gives them each a high-five.

"Wait," Roz says, lacing her fingers with Elise's. "I've got a better idea." From across the table, she bores her eyes into mine. "We don't need someone *in* the play. We need someone who's not in the play. The one who wants to work on the set with a hammer."

I give her a weird look, suddenly confused as to how I could possibly fit in this so-not-gonna-work-plan.

She leans forward, plants her hand on my shoulder, looks back at Elise. "Actors get all the glory, don't you think?" She clucks out the side of her mouth, tips her head back at mine. "How about focusing your camera behind the scenes?"

## Chapter 10

"Don't!" Reeta says, her arms outstretched to stop me from sitting.

I didn't stop; but I should have. I should have paid attention to her and not the new, comfy-looking chair I found in the living room. Because if I know anything, it's this: once you live with one ghost, you more or less come to live with them all. It takes all of two seconds for me to find we have a new one.

"Thanks for the warning," I say, jumping up from the chair, while rubbing the chill from my arms, my legs, my back.

"Warn you, I did," she says, slumping back into the white and blue flowered sofa. She straightens the black turban on her head. "But the wind was too strong for the trying. You might want to quell that storm you're carrying."

"Well, maybe we can use it to blow away Mom's latest visitor." I take another step away from the chair and edge into whatever warmth I can get from the afternoon sun working its way in through the windows.

Reeta Gertestky is Gram's best friend. Gram calls Reeta over whenever we have unwanted guests. Like now, apparently.

But I can see this one doesn't look like the usual floater that comes with Mom's corpses. He's not dressed in anything current. His suit is high-collared. His hat, tall and brimmed. His shoes, square, yet, so worn, the leather follows the shape of each toe. And his cane, which hooks down under his wrinkled hand, contrasts with a long, looping mustache, which curls up.

Reading my thoughts, Reeta shakes her head. "This one came with the chair.

"Internet order," she adds, as if that explains everything. Which, in a way, it does. Gram has a habit of shopping for antiques on eBay, and the new silver-striped chair must be what Gram calls an "Irresistible."

"So, this... *visitor* is going to need what? Relocation? Reincarnation? Post-visitation?" I feel like I've been stomped on. I mean, when did ghosts start arriving with furniture?

"Ah, Myri, you're home." Gram walks through the doorway from the kitchen.

Placing a tray of yellow butter cookies on the coffee table, she comes over to cup my face. Even without having seen her pink jacket and white slip-ons by the door, I know from the cool touch of her hands that she's been out for a walk.

"So, about the ghost?" I ask, while returning the hug that follows.

"Well, we don't know too much about him," Gram says, releasing me, "at least as far as where he wants to go, who he wants to see—he's not the talkative type."

I follow the ghost's gaze through a single, round eyeglass, held in place with a squint, toward the painting of water lilies hanging on the opposite side of the room. Whether he's studying it intently, or not at all, I can't tell. He could almost be mistaken for a statue, if it weren't for his wavering, see-through form, which shouts, Ghost!

I give a little huff, take a few steps back to sink into the rocker. "Didn't you buy a chair to sit in?"

"Well, yes," Gram says, bending to take a cookie.

"And has anyone sat it in, yet?"

Reeta presses her lips into a frown, scoffs with a wave of her hand, as Gram sits next to her. "Briefly," she says. "That's how we discovered he was there."

"And he's still there."

"Yes, because we don't know what he needs."

"He *needs* to move, that's what he needs." I'm finding it hard not to feel irritated.

"That'll happen, as soon as he gets up," Gram says matter-of-factly.

"Okaaaaay," I say, trying not to pull a face. "Am I the only one who sees a problem with this?"

I push myself up and turn a circle on the rug. "I mean, coming home to dead people—and sometimes ghosts that are linked to them—is one thing, because that's Mom's job. I can accept that. But coming home to find one stuck in a random piece of furniture you've just purchased? And seeing he's allowed to stay stuck until we can figure out *his needs*? That's something completely different. Aren't there like codes, or rules, or limits, or something?"

"Limits?" Gram tips her chin near her chest. "Of course, there are limits, Myri. We all know that. Along with a few doors, that open and close, on our side of reality and theirs. *Ours* happened *to be open* to him at the time."

Reeta leans forward and touches Gram's arm. "Well, we did direct that delivery man to bring him inside."

"But that was before we knew he was there."

"And now that you do know, don't you see a problem with it?" I say.

"Of course," Gram retorts.

"A *pressing* problem?"

"Of course, it's a pressing problem. I just haven't figured out how to help *him* see the problem." She sets her fists on her hips. "Where is all this coming from? We've dealt with this before, Myri. You know some cases take longer than others—the longest involving the one who lives upstairs. What's troubling you?"

I take a deep breath, hold it.

A lot is troubling me. A lot.

I lean forward and grab a cookie. "Have you seen Wren?"

58

 Chapter 11

Wren is sitting at the kitchen table, cupping her hands in a way that looks too familiar.

"What are you doing?"

I shake my head at the answer. She didn't have to tell me, and I didn't have to ask.

Energy balls.

She raises her brow in an innocent arch, as I stomp to the counter. "Mom," I say, keeping my tone curt, my voice flat. "Mom, tell her she's not going to school." I point at Wren, just to make sure she knows who I'm talking about.

She does, because her eyes wrinkle up like I'm nuts. But she doesn't glance my way until the last bit of leaf is peeled from the cob, which starts to worry me. "Wren," she finally says, drawing in a breath, "you're not to go to school."

*Yes!*

Wren's wail of protest drowns the room like one of the bells in Ardenport harbor.

"Now, why did I say that?" The sound of my mom's voice cuts through my short-lived triumph. She pivots to face me.

*She wasn't being serious.*

*How could she not have been serious?*

"Because she doesn't belong there. It's a school!"

Why is this concept hard to understand? It's not like we're talking about a younger sister, here. A real-live sibling, who, by law, should be in school, if she existed.

Mom picks up another ear of corn, peels back another faded green leaf, and another, before looking at me again, her face hard. "She could learn something at school. It *is* a public institution."

"Yea-ah. For people that are *living!*"

Are we really having this conversation? I had kind of hoped this request would be easy. No, not hoped. Expected. I had expected Wren would get in trouble.

"That depends on your definition of living, doesn't it?" She swoops a hand in Wren's direction. "Just because she doesn't have flesh and blood doesn't mean she doesn't exist." She shakes her head, caught in her own thoughts. "*Wren exists.* Simple as she's sitting there now." She presses a cob into my hands to peel. "If you exist, Myri, you live. Simple as that."

I chuck down the cob, grab a spoon off the counter. "Oh, yeah? Well, this spoon exists, Mom. That doesn't mean it lives."

Mom takes the spoon from my hand, waves it at Wren. "This spoon doesn't *think, feel*. Wren does. There's a difference."

I shake my head. "Well, would you be saying that, if you knew she helped Roz cheat? If you knew she did that by possessing Roz's body, so she could take a history test?"

Mom gasps, turns a horrified look on Wren. "Was Roz okay?"

At least she agrees *that's* wrong.

Wren pushes her mouth into a frown. "It wasn't that long a time."

"Well." Mom rubs her hand along the edge of the counter, takes in a deep breath, then takes her time blowing it out. "Wren," she finally says, "I don't want you doing that again. It's not right. It could be dangerous."

"Going to school is too, obviously."

"And you," she says, pointing her finger at me, "you really ought to have told me as soon as you knew what had happened."

"But I did!"

Mom shakes her head. "Not entirely. Not at first. You started out talking about this not going to school business."

I let out an exasperated huff. "Yuh, okay, whatever, but this means she can't go anymore, right? It should, shouldn't it?"

"No, I didn't say that—" Mom curses under her breath, checks her watch, looks at the water bubbling on the stove. "Girls, you're going to have to finish dinner yourselves."

"*I'm* going to have to finish, you mean. Wren doesn't eat."

"You know what I mean." She unties her apron in a fluster. "I forgot the Andersons are coming to go over the arrangements for Luella's wake tomorrow. They'll be here any minute. And I'm not dressed. *Luella's not dressed.*" She pushes her hands through her hair, swearing three more times under her breath. "Why did I stop to buy corn?"

"I don't know, maybe you were possessed?"

Mom doesn't reply.

Instead, she marches to the foot of the stairs. "And you're in charge of Wren tonight," she says, stopping in the doorway.

"What? Wait! Why? Gram can watch her!"

"Gram..." She waves her arm at the living room, "Gram is busy at the moment, as I'm sure you noticed."

"But I have a drama meeting! At the theater! Don't tell me she's allowed to go there!"

"Oh, that's right." Mom tsks, pats the door frame, as my internal alarms start blaring.

"You know about the meeting?"

"Yes," she says, keeping her eyes on the frame, pretending to give it an inspection. "Charles told me about it earlier."

*Charles!?!*

"He wants me to organize costumes."

"Wait—what?"

Her eyes flicker, as they briefly meet mine.

I grab my head to keep it from spinning. This can't be happening. Not because of some stupid project I did with bugs.

"You—you're not going to do the costumes, are you?"

"Why do you say that? Of course, I am. Why wouldn't I? You're involved, so I want to be involved. It'll be a way for us to spend more time together."

More time with him, you mean.

Reading my look of disgust, Mom raises a stiff hand. "I don't have time for this, Myr. But as far as tonight goes, you're taking Wren with you."

"I don't want to take her with me."

"You don't have a choice. She can't be here."

"*What?*"

"Look, I don't care what you do, just work it out somehow."

And with that warm bit of news and advice, she runs up the stairs, leaving me with Wren in the kitchen.

It takes all of a second to realize I'm only a few yards from the lab.

Maybe I'll trade places with Luella.

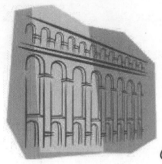

Chapter 12

Working it out was getting Roz to watch her, then strapping a headlamp to my handlebars (safety counts!), so I could bike to Ardenport Community Theater. It's about three miles from my house, which has given me three miles to grumble about Roz. Because even though she's helping me out, she's making me pay her.

That's right. Pay her.

For babysitting a ghost.

Like she isn't going to have a good time.

They're probably possessing each other right now.

To practice taking more tests in history. Or, maybe to help Roz skip school altogether.

Well. At least *I* know where to draw the line.

I'd decided that almost as soon as Roz made her suggestion.

I still can't believe Roz let Wren do that. Couldn't she have just whispered the answers? Or, would that have been too simple? I'll have to point that out for next time.

*Listen to me. Next time.*

I park my bike in the rack at the front of the theater and assure myself once again, that yes, I can do this. I can walk inside, find a seat, and read my lines. I've got six. I think I handle reading six.

Or not.

Because as soon as I walk through the double glass doors, the breath I'm holding for luck and protection rushes out of me when I step inside. The lobby is enormous. The dark maroon carpet that covers the floor stretches for an eternity toward four sets of gold-rimmed, white-paneled doors, one of which stands open like an ominous maw. Without any real lifelines within reach—like the arm of a friend—I feel like a guppy floundering a blood-red sea.

Cass has picked a bad night to be late. She was supposed to be waiting at the entrance, but she isn't. Nor is she standing among any of the groups huddled in the lobby.

Wonderful.

Somehow, I make my way in, following the last of the late-comers. Their path leads me to a seat at the end of the third row. It's not until I'm planted that I realize I've sat directly behind Blow-it-out-of-proportion-Brittley.

"The color red is so out for me this year," she says, ranting to Londyn. "An article in *Glam* said red makes you *eat more*. Can you believe that? So, I went to my closet and threw away everything that was red—well, I didn't exactly throw everything away. I put the clothes in a bag for the poor, because you know, poor people are hungry all the time, so they don't mind eating more."

*Say what?*

"But not me. No, for me, it's all about blue. Blue is the color that makes you eat less."

"Oh, I love blue," Londyn replies. "I've always loved blue."

"Me, too," Brittley says. "But now, I *have* to. If I gain even one pound, my agent will kill me."

"Plus, blue looks good on you. You should wear it, even if it didn't make you diet."

Brittley tips her head, lets out a knowing sigh. "You're so right, Londyn. Even if it didn't come with benefits, I'd still wear it. That and pink. Pink's never been my favorite, but according to *Glam*, it makes food taste sweeter."

On hearing this—despite my anxiety of what's in store for the evening, or perhaps, because of it—I snort, which unfortunately, for want-to-go-unnoticed-me, comes out louder than I intended. In less than the snap of two manicured fingertips, Brittley spins in her seat to give me a glare. She nudges Londyn for attention.

Not caring what she might say, or think, I cup my hand dramatically behind my ear.

"First of all," Brittley says, with a roll of her eyes. "I can't believe you actually have the guts to sit here, after that whole cockroach-volcano thing. If I'd known what Mr. Slayer was thinking, I would have had made a point to talk to him. Get him to put

66

you in another club. Spare us the pain and suffering that your presence seems to bring, because there's no way that you, of all people, will do anything good for the play. In fact, I'm sure, if given a chance, you'll find a way to ruin it. So, let's be clear, shall we? I'm all in agreement for you working behind the scenes."

"Great. So am I."

"Great. But just because we have one thing we agree on, doesn't mean we're friends. So, from now on, *find another perch.*" She wiggles her fingertips. "Take your bad luck—or, charm—or, whatever it is—somewhere else. Don't sit behind me."

Diggs claps once, twice, three times from the other side of the stage. "It looks like nearly everyone is here. Shall we begin?" He holds his arms out, walks a small circle. "Pretty impressive, don't you think?" He points down at the stage around him.

Actually, despite the company I can't seem to avoid, it is. At least as far as theaters go. Not that I would know, since I've never really been in this one, or any other for that matter, other than the one at school, which doesn't count.

The stage in the school gym is nothing compared to this one with its plush, maroon-velvet seats that wrap around the stage in curved, rising rows.

And the ceiling, painted with a mural of angels and other heavenly-looking people wearing crowns, flowers, and togas, along with towering white pillars give the feeling of sitting in an ancient Roman cathedral.

Diggs brings his arms in, smiles at everyone. "I can't tell you how excited I am to announce—or *re-announce*, as it is—the support that Ardenport Community Theater is giving our production by allowing us to put on our play here."

Diggs pauses to lead everyone in a polite applause, while gesturing toward a silver-haired woman in the front row who stands and takes a bow.

"Given the size and scope of what we are about to undertake, this stage will offer everything we need and more.

"*And* because this is a professional theater, I'm asking each of you to be on your best behavior while using these facilities."

Best behavior? You got it. Let me be part of the audience. I'll be the best-behaved theater-goer Wolford has ever seen. In fact, being a member of the audience should be an option for club participation. I could help fill a seat. Make it a full house. Isn't that what theaters are always striving for, anyway? A full house? And I could do one thing better. I could lead the audience—clap, gasp, laugh, cry—always on cue. And always with the utmost affection.

Diggs rubs his hands in front of his chest. "Now, what I'd like you all to do is move out of your seats—*slowly,* please, *carefully*—and join me up here on the stage." He raises his hands by his sides, gesturing us to stand.

I wait to get up, giving Brittley and Londyn lots of time to move ahead.

"That's it. Upt! Hold it!" Diggs walks briskly to the opposite side of the stage. "Let me point out that there are *two* sets of stairs that can be used, so if some of you would travel to *stage-left*, that would help us move smoothly and without harm. We're not looking to have anyone fall and break a leg. Not tonight!"

Like an obedient, if not sluggish cow, I join half the herd, and head toward the stairs at what must be stage-left.

"Good. Thank you to those who helped alleviate the congestion. Please, gather at the center of the stage….Center stage. Right here, around me."

Despite my efforts to separate myself from Brittley and company, I find myself standing behind her again, but unable to move since now I'm trapped in the middle of the crowd. How did I get in the middle? I should be on the side. No, the sidelines. Way, way, way, over there. Behind that curtain.

Fanning the lapels of his brown tweed jacket, Diggs starts talking again. "I hope you've all taken time to look over the scenes I selected for auditions. We'll begin reading through them tonight."

Some kids gasp, as if this is new information, others chatter with delight.

Diggs pats his hands in the air. "We talked about this in class, so you should be aware of what's happening. *Furthermore*, let me point out that this is an excellent opportunity to get a feel for the stage and allow you to envision your place on it. Our time at this facility will be limited, so I want you to make

69

the most of it, while we are here. Look around. Come to know how the stage is laid out, how it feels to be up here, facing an audience." He swoops his arms out toward the empty seats—*three floors of them*.

"Visualization of the mind is a very powerful thing," he adds. "Use it to your advantage."

Uh, we need to rethink that, because the thought of being up here in front of an audience, even a small one, is making me ill.

"But, to do that, I suppose we need to get to work." Diggs spins back around, holds up sheets of paper. "Anyone forget to bring these? Our script?" A few hands go up, including mine, but I don't step forward to get one. Brittley and Londyn are blocking my path, engaged in a loud, squealish conversation.

"You're dating him? He asked you?"

Brittley rolls her eyes to the ceiling, rests her weight back on one foot.

"No-ooo. He didn't ask. Why would I wait for him to do that? *I just told him*. I said, 'Hey, we should go out.' It's not like I expected him to say no. After all, it makes perfect sense. He's in drama, I'm in drama. I'll get the lead, he'll get the lead...."

I have no idea who Brittley is talking about, nor do I care; but when she lets out a happy gasp, I can't stop myself from turning to see who has come.

Chapter 13

"Myri!" Diggs calls.

I don't move. Of all the people Brittley could have been talking about, why did it have to be him?

"Myri!" Diggs flutters a script in his hands, strides across the stage. "Didn't you have a hand up for one of these?"

"Uh... yeah."

"Then, here. Take it. I'm sure you've got some reviewing to do." Turning on his toes, he pauses, holding his now empty hand in the air. "Oh, and I know you were hinting in class that you wanted to be assigned to the set crew, but those positions are rather limited. When we bought the rights to the play from Theaters Unlimited, we rented props and a set to go with it. So, nothing needs to be built. And the technical staff of Ardenport Theater will be assisting."

He holds a hand to his mouth, as if sharing a secret. "They really don't want kids messing with their equipment. Lighting, sound, etcetera...." He rubs his hand at the back of his neck, then pats his face, as if thinking. "So," he says, setting his eyes back on me, "I'd really like you to focus your efforts on auditions. Nearly everyone will be given roles in the play."

"But—!"

Diggs holds up a hand. "I look forward to seeing how you do, Myri. After all, you may surprise yourself. I, for one, believe we all have hidden talents." He takes a step back, pulls his chin into his chest, tips up a bushy sideburn. "Never walk away from doors presented to you."

I open my mouth to speak, but Diggs raises finger. "Upt! No excuses. Especially now that your partner is here."

"Partner?"

He points.

I turn to find Duey, Brittley's new boyfriend, standing behind me. He leans forward. "To think we almost got out of this."

"Uh, yeah," I manage, not knowing quite what he means. *Shouldn't he be standing with Brittley?*

Skirting his chocolate-brown eyes from mine, he directs a quick nod across the stage. Brittley returns it with a smile that tries to say, "It's okay, you can talk to anyone you like." But all actors have their limits, and it seems this situation has exposed hers.

Duey pivots to give me a nudge, sending a volt of electricity straight from my gut to the back of my heart. "Slayer told me one day we'd appreciate the fact that he cared."

I begin to make sense of what he's saying. "You got kicked out of study hall, too?" My voice barely manages a whisper.

He shakes his head proudly. "Yep."

I don't know why, but this makes me feel better. Like we're linked by the cosmos in some way. "Well, I'd have appreciated it more, if I could have been put in art class."

Duey shrugs, looks around. "Drama's not so bad."

"Maybe not for you. You did this last year, didn't you?"

Diggs clears his throat, pulls a script from under his arm. "Sorry to interrupt, Myri, Duey, but as I said, our time is short. Since you're paired together, you may want to practice. Duey, do you need one of these?"

I study his face, as he takes the script, expecting it to fill with horror as the idea of *who his partner is* settles in. But it doesn't. Instead, his face shows something more like pleasant surprise.

Misreading my confusion, Diggs blurts, "Did I not mention partners?" He spins around, raises his arms in the air. "People! People! Eyes, ears over here! This is very important! I can see that some of you are looking over the script with friends, which is fine. But, *please*, take note that I've assigned partners for the actual auditions, which we'll start in fifteen minutes. *Therefore*, it may be to your *benefit* to take time to prepare with her, or him."

Diggs makes a point to look back at me, before scurrying to a table at the back of the stage.

"But, Mr. Diggs!" Brittley cries, running to him. He continues to shuffle through a stack of papers. "Every audition I've ever done has been alone for the first reading."

"Yes, yes, that may be true," he says, continuing to shuffle and sort. "But let me share what makes this experience different." He looks up at her. "One, this is a drama class. And two, our time is limited. We've got a few weeks before opening night. Therefore, I've structured the auditions to be a learning opportunity to meet the first point, while making them run as efficiently as possible to meet the second. It's my hope that when we are done, we'll be able to say that although not everyone will have been cast in big roles in the play, at least everyone will have had the chance to read from a scene as if they were in one."

"But—!"

"Ah, here they are." He waves a blue paper over his head, dismissing her protest. "Your partner assignments. Pass this around, so everyone can see."

Stepping from the swarm, Diggs makes his way back to the thick, velvet folds of the closing curtain, where I've escaped.

"So, Myri," he says, polishing his fingernails on his shirt pocket. "To be clear, if you haven't already figured it out, you'll be reading with Mr. Williams. But I'll have you do it tomorrow morning, during class, since you've both had such short notice. We'll

74

be using the stage in the gym for that." He juts his chin to where Duey is standing with Cam. "I think it's for the best. Like you, he's another student who was just added to the club."

Club... class... what does it matter?

Either way, I'm doomed.

Chapter 14

Duey.

Save him? Or, don't save him?

Those are the questions I've been asking.

Because he does need to be saved. And not just from Brittley, but from my complete stupidity.

Let me explain.

Obviously, Brittley thinks she has her plans all worked out with thinking she and Duey will be spending time together in the play, which theoretically, wouldn't be a problem. I could easily ruin that with my audition—*I.E.*, if I look bad, Duey will look bad, which means Diggs will have to give another guy the leading role.

BUT! Duey wants the leading role! I heard him talking to Cam about it. So, if I screw that up for him, then I'm never going to meet my own secret goal of getting Duey for myself when Roz gets over him. Last I checked, looking like an idiot in an audition isn't part of *Teen Life's* top ten list for "How To Get a Boy to Like You."

Plus, it may not even be necessary to keep Duey and Brittley apart. It doesn't seem to me that he's all that into her. He didn't talk to her much at the theater. I even asked him about it—only because I was getting so confused. I said, "I hear you're going out with Brittley." (I had to know the truth—for Roz's sake.)

And he said, "Yeah, so she tells me." I chuckled along with him, my hopes rising.

"So, it's true, then?"

He squirmed. "It's true, I guess."

I nodded, feeling kind of let down that Duey would let someone like Brittley control him like that. "So, any girl could tell you that you're going out with her, and you'd be okay with that?"

"Sure."

But I didn't believe him, and to prove he was wrong, I pushed the point. "So, I could tell you right now, 'we're going out,' and you'd say, 'okay?'"

He tipped his head, raised his brow. He might have even blushed. (If he was embarrassed, I didn't care. I wanted him to see how ridiculous he was being.) But instead of saying, 'You're right, it's not true that anyone could come up and say that and expect me go along with it,' he smiled and said, "Well, you're not just anyone. It'd be more than okay."

*It'd be more than okay?*

*!?!?!?*

He wasn't supposed to say that.

Well, *it was nice to hear*, but my point was supposed to get him to dump Brittley, so that Roz could have another chance with him.

Which leaves me with my new problem. When it comes to saving Duey, from whom am I saving him, exactly?

Brittley?

Or, me?

## Chapter 15

"Myri? I believe you're next."

My stomach replies with a violent heave, making me curl slightly.

My mind reels. I have no idea how I'm going to get myself up from the floor.

I wish I'd skipped class, skipped auditions. Taken the F.

An F would be so much more bearable than crumbling alongside Duey up on stage.

Diggs rolls his fingers in an impatient wave from the center of the gym. Everyone else is scattered along the walls, under the hoops, and on the bleachers. Cass gives me a friendly push, as I roll to my knees, which I suppose, is helpful. After all, I'm shaking so badly, I can barely stand.

Inching my way toward the Lime Light of Doom, I'm hit with an idea. Maybe I can get credit for auditioning as a rock, or a log, or something that doesn't talk or move. I can roll up in a ball, and Duey can sit on my back, while he reads his lines.

"Take it from the top of page three, please," Diggs says, when I step on stage.

Okay, page 3... page 3....

I tap my head. I can't remember if there's a rock on page 3.

Paper rustles, and from the corner of my eye, I see Duey tuck his script in his pocket.

Wait—he's memorized his lines? Already?

Sweat breaks on my brow, as the tunnel I've just fallen in grows at warp speed.

I'm going to faint.

I'm moving a zillion miles away, and I'm going to faint.

I can't faint. Not here. Not now.

"Myri?"

Did Duey say his first line?

What's his line? What's at the top of page 3? I pat my pockets, both front and back. I don't have a script. How can I not have my script? I look out at the theater, looking for Cass, looking for a clue. Diggs is leaning forward, almost grimacing, waiting for words to be spoken.

I rub my cheek. My face feels hot, my palms wet.

"Is no one here?"

Okay. Now I know this is the second time Duey has said this. He takes a step sideways, as if looking for someone, which is what he should be doing. After all, he's the prince, and he's looking for me in this scene, the owner of the bakery.

"Uh—" My words fall short in my mouth. I can almost feel them there, fighting to get out, trying to say what I need to say, which is something like, 'What is it you could possibly seek in a place such as this? It's been a hundred moons since someone has stopped by.'

I'm supposed to say this, while trying to hide as the poor, dismally-cursed Nelle.

I'd like to hide now.

"Uh," I try again. But the words don't come. I stare at the back of Duey's head, and wonder what he must be thinking.

Brittley lets out a guffaw. Duey drops his arms by his sides, looks questioningly out at Diggs. I've totally goofed it.

"Uh, could you excuse me a moment?" I've finally found my voice. "I just remembered... I need... Uh... my cell phone. I'll be right back."

I jump off the stage.

Diggs jumps from his seat. "Wait. Where are you going?" His clipboard clatters to the floor. "Is everything all right?"

"Yeah," I lie, leaving wet streaks where my hands rub my jeans. "I'll be back in a minute."

## Chapter 16

The coolness of the brick wall outside the gymnasium door presses through my shirt, and I realize I've forgotten my sweater and my binder. I'm going to have to go back in there.

Great. As if avoiding a slow and painful death once in one day isn't enough, I'll have to somehow manage it all over again.

But not yet. Footsteps draw my attention down the hall.

Roz.

"What are you doing out here?" she asks. "Did we miss it? Is your audition done?"

I let out a huff, look away, look back. "What am I doing here? What are you doing here? Or, more importantly—" My eyes adjust to the shadowy figure beside her. "What's *she* doing here?"

Wren floats a little higher. "We came to be cheering y' on. Mrs. Haines thinks Roz is in the bathroom."

I scoff. "Well, there's no need for that." I pull the black elastic out of my hair, shake out the ponytail, then pull it all back again. "I made a total fool of myself. Hopefully, Duey's not still gaping on stage."

"You read your lines with Duey?" Roz's voice goes weak with hope.

I shake my head. "I barely muttered a syllable."

She sets an ear on her shoulder, trying to dip her head lower to meet my eyes. "Well, was it a good syllable?"

She's trying to be funny, but I don't laugh.

Wren slips closer. "Surely, ye said more than that. Even a newborn babe can let out a sound or two, when it opens its mouth."

"Nope."

Roz throws up her hands. "Myri, you have to go back in there and read your lines."

"No way."

"But you'll fail. And Brittley will get the part with Duey, which will make things worse than they already are!"

I bump my head back against the wall. "Well, there's nothing I can do about that."

"Okay, okay. So maybe you won't keep Brittley from getting the lead, but you'll fail with your grade. Even if Diggs is dating your mother."

"Maybe I should fail then. Maybe my mom will get mad and stop seeing him."

Roz shakes her head, looks at me, looks at Wren, then back at me again. "Why don't you let Wren help. Then you'll be able to get through the trimester banging nails on the set like you want."

I ignore the nodding head that's floating beside her.

"Diggs is going to make you do it, anyway," she argues. "Just go in there and get it over with. While you still can. And while Wren is here to do it with you."

Wren gives a faint smile—one that has more strength than I'm able to manage. Her gaze goes to the window pane of the gym door. The light streaming out from it almost seems to reflect back a glow of confidence in her hazy form.

"There's nothing to it, Myr," Wren says, setting her gray eyes on mine. "Truly, there's not an easier thing to be done. Just let me pull ye along, like a puppet on a string. Could be a wee bit of fun, I imagine. I've never set foot in a theater—or, on a stage, I mean—but I think I've always been wanting to try."

I look to Roz, let out a defeated breath. "Like a puppet on a string?"

Roz nods. "All you have to do is sit back and enjoy the ride."

 Chapter 17

"Yer trying harder than ye ought."

Wren's voice rings through my head, because that's where she is. In my head, my arms, my legs, my chest. It's a good thing I haven't eaten peas lately, because this brings back bad memories.

"Like a puppet on a string," Roz says encouragingly.

I almost want to hit her for talking me into doing this, and I would, if I had any control over my body, which I don't. Because if I did, I wouldn't be walking like this—not with my legs and arms swinging out with each step....

I mean, what does Wren think she's doing? Does she really think people walk like this? This is Roz's solution? Handing myself over to a nitwit of a ghost?!

"Of course," Wren says, pressing her hands—*my hands*—to my hips.

I slap my hand over my mouth in surprise. I hadn't expected Wren to read my thoughts, to *respond* to them with her own.

And my voice…. It has an Irish lilt to it.

Wren nods my head, answering my thoughts once again.

"I hadn't counted on this being so invasive," I mutter more at Roz, than Wren.

"And I hadn't counted on these clothes being so tight," Wren retorts.

"Well, you're not wearing your ratty nightgown anymore, so you can stop walking like you are!"

"Myr!" Roz says, wiggling her hands by her ears in frustration. "One of you talking is more than enough. You've got to trust Wren to do the work. You've got to let her do everything for you. If you go in there fighting it, especially when Wren is trying to walk—" she takes a step back as she looks at me, shakes her head, "then Diggs will think you skipped down to the Bill's Pub and Brewery."

"Okay, okay. Just give me a second. Both of you."

I close my eyes, take a deep breath, and slowly let it out. I try to imagine letting go of my body. Letting go and stepping away.

Amazingly, after a moment, it feels like I do, although I don't step, exactly. I float. Barely. A little, off to the side. Yet, somehow, I'm still hinged. I'm separate, but not.

I can see myself standing here, but at the same time, I know it's not me…. It looks like me. But it's Wren. This is so weird. What makes it Wren?

She moves my arm, and a second later, as if there's a time-lapse, I feel her moving it for me.

Well. *I'll say this.* Nothing I've ever done compares.

*This* is detachment on a whole new level. In a whole new dimension. Because I'm seeing how I look from the outside. How everyone else sees me. And I'm not sure I like it.

Wren swivels my hips. "I think we're ready for a dance on me trotters."

*What?*

Before I can find a way to stop her, Wren opens the door and marches us in.

## Chapter 18

The weight of thirty stares falls on me, as I re-enter the gym, making me forget about staying let-go. Muted snickers rattle my ears. My heart catches in my throat. And suddenly, I find myself struggling, once again, to breathe.

I have to do this. I can do this.

"No, ye don't," Wren hisses. "Yer supposed to be leaving that to me."

Oh. Right….

"Myri," Diggs says, shifting in his seat to look at me. "I'm so glad you're back. Feeling refreshed, I hope? Would you like another shot at your lines?"

Wren nods my head, as she takes me a bit less swaggery toward the stage. When we pass Diggs, I feel myself turn and bend at the knees.

*Was that a curtsy?*

This is followed by an excited little hop.

*Please, don't do that.*

"I would love to be reading my lines, with all the thanks of a thousand souls, although I've only got me one," Wren says with a giggle.

*And drop the Irish accent!*

Wren tips her head, and turns a small circle, looking at the banners, the bleachers on the far wall, the shiny wood floor.

*And stop looking like you've never been here before!*

She smiles at Diggs. "I'll be ready, now that all the nerves are stopped jumping in me gullet."

*Stop talking like that!*

"Err, great," Diggs says, arching his brow. "No apologies necessary. Duey? Would you mind taking the stage?"

"Sure." He jumps up from the floor, lifts his blue baseball cap, and puts the visor at the back of his head, leaving tufts of brown hair sticking through the band at the front.

Wren takes in a quick breath, which makes me take in a quick breath, which makes us cough and splutter.

*That there would be Duey?*

*Ye-aah! Now, follow him to the stage.*

*But don't skip!*

We careen to a stop in front of him.

Wren brings my hand to rest on my chin, as she looks out at Diggs. "Would there be a script-thingy handy?"

Duey turns his mouth up in a grin, takes the script from his pocket, steps closer. "Just take a deep breath," he whispers, turning his back to the gym. "Follow my lead, and we'll both get through this. Unless, of course, you want to ditch me again. Twice in one day would be a first, although I'm always up for new things. I just don't think an F should be yours." He stands back and shows me another smile.

With a short, nervous laugh, Wren darts a glance in his direction. She pats my sides, straightens my shoulders. "Don't y' be worrying yer head over a silly thing such as that."

Right.

"Now, where were we...."

*The bakery scene! Page 3!*

"Oh, yes." Wren flips to the right page and reads the scene's description. "The run-down bakery. Where Prince Bastian meets Nelle, who's been living alone as a cursed, hunch-backed, half-human goat.... Oh, my." She looks out at Diggs. "Should I be hunching me-self over for this? Like an ill-begotten goat?"

He laughs, I presume, at the way I sound. She hasn't bothered to soften the Irish accent. "Uh, no. Reading it will be fine."

She looks at Duey, or rather, we look at Duey, who smiles and takes a half-step forward.

"Is no one here?" He pauses, and then turns away, as if he doesn't see me.

"No. No, there be no one," Wren replies, making my voice raspy, while throwing it off to the side, as if she were hiding behind a barrel, like the script says.

"Surely, you're mistaken," Duey replies.

"No.... But I dare say it's been a hundred moons since anyone has crossed my threshold. What is it

90

ye could possibly seek in a place as low and empty as this?"

"The one attached to that sweet voice."

Wren huffs like the script says. "Sire, either yer brain has grown daft, or else cast under the spell of a bad fairy, if ye thinks me craggy voice, weighted with the age of a hundred years, sounds sweet to human ears. Twould be better if ye left, and never returned."

Duey shakes his head. "I have no way, nor desire, to leave this place. The skies have grown dark. The air, heavy with foreboding. Please, my maiden, believe me when I say I can hear the kindness in your voice. Take mercy and offer me some bread, if not some company. For it has been many a day I've been lost in the forest. My stomach has grown weak with hunger. My heart, weary with loneliness."

Tucking the script under my arm, Wren begins moving my hands in front of me, as if hastily stacking a tray with food. A few moments later, she shoves the imaginary tray forward, then opens the script again.

"'Tis only hard bread I can offer today." She pushes forward an imaginary pitcher. "And water. But yer belly won't be thanking me for it. Despite me efforts to knead the yeast through, me loafs refuse to rise. Forgive me, but 'tis the best I can do."

Duey pretends to take a bite. A tough bite, but one that shows growing pleasure at the taste. When it comes to acting, he's actually pretty good.

"Who makes such fine food? The taste belies its sight. It would be lovely with a spot of tea. Show yourself. Come sit with me a while. We'll heat a kettle by the fire."

"Y' don't know what y' ask. Please, eat and be on yer way!" Wren tips my head, as if spying on Prince Bastian from behind an imaginary curtain. "There be evil lurking in these woods!"

Finally, with a spin, a bow, and a flirty wave, Wren gives us quick leave of the stage.

"That was great!" Roz says.

Only Roz would have the courage to sneak backstage, when she's not even supposed to be here.

Wren lets out a long-winded breath from my mouth. "Well, I'd trade all the gold of Ireland to know what Duey'll be thinking."

We turn to see him give a thumbs up, as he makes his way off the other side of the stage. Even though I'm not completely connected to my body, I feel the full force of my stomach going queasy.

"Okay, that's it. Time for you to leave." I stretch my arms up to shake Wren free, squeeze my eyes shut.

With a slight fluttering from my belly—as if we're being pulled apart like string cheese—Wren appears before me, looking like the ghost she's always been.

"Feel better?" Roz asks, draping her arm across my shoulders.

"Like I've been bathed in the breath of life," Wren says.

I brush at my arms, making sure all of me is still here, give Wren a hard squint. "She was asking me, Genius. And we're never doing that again."

Chapter 19

I'm hanging my jacket in my locker—and still humming, of all things (something I've done since last Friday)—when Roz and Elise come running down the hall. Elise reaches me first. "I can't believe it, Myr! You did it!"

"Did what?"

Roz slides behind and gives me a push. "Come on! You'll see!"

They pull me with them, not caring how many kids we bump along the way. At the end of the next corridor, they push me head-long through a crowd of students gathered around the bulletin board outside Diggs's door.

"It's the cast and crew list," Elise says.

"Yeah, so?"

"Wellllll, check it out!" The sound of Roz's voice makes me believe I'm about to read the best-news-ever. I mean, why would she be happy, if not to show I've gotten what I wanted. A behind-the-scenes assignment. Maybe Diggs teamed me up with my mom. It'd make sense for him to put us together. And if that's the case, I'd be more than happy to help. Happy enough to do ALL the work. Let her stay home.

But my name isn't among the list of assignments for costumes.

Confused, I look back at Roz and Elise, who hook arms with Cass, as she steps between them. They jut their chins at the list, urging me to look again.

I re-read—slower this time—going up from the bottom. No, I'm not with the set crew, nor hair and make-up. Nor lights and music…. Is there another page?… No. Just this one.

The color slowly drains from my face. My skin goes cold and clammy. My eyes slowly move their way to the top.

I'm not a tree.

Not a soldier.

Not a townsfolk 3, 2, or 1.

Not the witch's cat.

"Here!" Roz says, jumping over me to plant her finger near the top of the list. "Here you are! Somehow, someway… you're Nelle!"

Oh, *no*.

A thousand pricks of electricity burst over my skin.

She's right.

How can she be right?

But there it is. Second from the top, under Prince Bastian, who's being played by Duey, I see it.

My name. In black letters. Next to the character of Nelle.

I read it again.

Nelle: Myri Monaco.

"Isn't it awesome?!" Cass says, pumping her fists with a squeal. "You got the lead! You beat Brittley!"

## Chapter 20

"Nonsense!" Diggs says, turning from his computer. "You were wonderful! *Wonderful!*"

My face scrunches up in disbelief. "Were we even at the same audition?"

"Of course! Of course, we were!"

"But I can't act. You saw me. I ran out of the theater. When I get in front of people for presentations or anything involving speaking, I choke up."

"No, I don't think so."

"But I will. I know I will."

"You won't. You'll be perfect."

"I'd rather be perfect at something that doesn't involve speaking. If I have to be in the play, cast me as a tree."

Diggs shakes his head, gives a wave of his hand. "All this talk about trees.... It'd be foolish to waste your talent."

"No, it wouldn't! I'd love that."

He grimaces. "Myri, listen. I'll admit, you started with a few jitters, but that's normal. It didn't last long. After you came back to the stage, you carried Nelle's role off perfectly. I loved the nuances, the accent, the mannerisms, how everything flowed so smoothly together.

"You stepped so completely into character. It was as if you weren't even there. And that, my dear, is rare, for someone so new to acting. You have natural talent. And it would be a crime, if I didn't reward it." He pauses, looks at me warmly. "You have a gift, Myri. You let yourself fade away and allowed Nelle, our heroine, to shine through. It was amazing to watch. It took my breath away. It still does, when I think of it."

"But it—but that—it was a fluke! I want to be on the set crew! Or costumes! Put me with my mother on costumes."

He opens his hands. "I imagine your mother would love for you to pitch in—that is, if you have time. But, Myri, plays hinge on the performers who play the leads. You are an example of a strong performer. A thespian, whom the rest will follow. You'll bring out the best in everyone. It will amount to a fine set of performances all around."

"But—"

"I'm really quite hopeful this will be the best play we've done."

"But what about Brittley?"

"Brittley has been cast in a fine role. She'll make a great witch. A good witch is hard for any actor to pull off. She'll need to be not only believable in her role, but likeable, despite all the bad things her character says and does. Being able to pull that off is very important in keeping the audience engaged throughout the show. I dare say, Brittley has a fair bit of work cut out for herself. I've already talked to her about it, and she's willing to take on such a challenge. That is why we need you to play the part of Nelle."

"We?"

"We." Mr. Diggs gives a curt nod. "Me. The club. The school. The theater...." He pauses. "I didn't want to tell anyone this, but the theater has been struggling financially for some time. If things don't turn around soon, this may be the beginning of the end for Ardenport Community Theater. Part of ACT's partnering with us has been done with all good intentions and hopes of bringing in new patrons. Young patrons and their families. And by all means, as I see now, new talent.

"You, Myri, are new talent. Exciting talent.

"And new, exciting talent always brings new life to a theater." He rubs his hands together. "So, not only is Wolford Academy depending on you, Ardenport Community Theater is depending on you. Everyone in the play will be depending on you. As will I be depending on you to elevate the entire performance."

Diggs's eyes grow distant, his hands pause in the air. "Let's just say I couldn't have asked for more in an audition. Because if what I saw a few days ago indicates what you can do with a first-time experience on the stage,... *Watch out!*" He snaps his fingers. "I know there are only better things to come."

Chapter 21

Better things have not come.

In drama, we spent the morning acting like animals. Literally. To teach us how to deal with embarrassing situations when we find ourselves feeling like idiots—like those never-ending moments when we're acting in front of hundreds of people....

I couldn't even howl in front of twenty-nine.

Because that was my assignment. To howl like a hyena.

And then, when I asked to be excused to the bathroom? I was told to stay in character.

Uh, yeah. Like I was going to lift my leg, so I could pee like a wild dog.

And now at lunch, Cass is wagging her finger over her milk at me, saying, "You know, Myri, you say, 'I can't do this,' a lot. But you know what? Based on what I saw last Friday, I hate to tell you, but you can. I think Diggs made the right choice. You were good. Especially when you thought what you did wouldn't matter. Maybe you need to stop worrying so much."

I look at Roz, but even though she knows what *really* happened in that audition, she says, "Cass is right, Myri. I mean, look how well it worked out. For one thing, you'll get a passing grade."

"Oh, great, and for another thing?"

She takes a bite of cinnamon roll, talks around her food as she chews. "Well, Duey isn't paired with Brittley, so he's safe."

Safe? My mouth drops.

A snort erupts from the end of the table, where Brittley is examining her red-tipped fingernails. "Actually, Roz, I couldn't agree more, which is really quite surprising, all things considered."

Twirling her hands down, Brittley parks them on the studded, black belt at her hips and presses her chest forward through a white, buttoned shirt. "Yes, Duey is *safe*. Because after he's done rolling his eyes at every pathetic thing Myri says *and does*, as she *tries* to act out her role of a goat—." Brittley pauses to sneer, then raises her voice to a sickly lilt.

"You did read the play, didn't you, Myri? For the entire play, until the very last scene, you're dressed as a goat. Because the witch—hah, *me!*—has a fabulous touch." She tosses her head, brushes her hand on her shoulder. "So, with everything you'll be bungling during your performance, combined with that lovely costume you'll have to wear, Duey will have no where else to look, but at me. And for a witch, I won't be looking all that bad."

She fixes a cold gaze on Roz. "So, I agree. From one girl to another, you're right. He's safe with Myri."

Cass drops her fork and stands to meet Brittley at eye level. "Oh, I'd say he's *safe*. But the facts in your fantasy are a bit off. Because after all's said and done, after Myri and Duey have spent all that time practicing and reading their lines together—out of costume, I might add—sharing those romantic moments, sharing that *last... romantic... kiss....*" Cass pauses. Roz seems to catch a small bug in her throat. Brittley's eyes flutter.

And in the space of that silence? My brain does a flip in my skull.

*Kiss?*

Cass smiles. "Yeah, kiss," she says, reading Brittley's face. "The costume isn't going to matter. She has to wear it, how long? For a few hours during dress rehearsal and the play?

"So, yeah, you can strut your witchy-stuff anyway you want, but Duey isn't going to be interested in looking anywhere, but here." Cass points down on top of my head, leans toward Roz, whispering, "Sorry, I'm just saying...."

Roz shrugs, gives me a thankful look. "Sure. Myri will be awesome, at whatever needs to be done."

Cass looks Brittley up and down, lets a slow smile curl on her face. "Think about that, why don't you, while you're rehearsing for your role of a wicked, old witch."

Uh... did she say, kiss?

Chapter 22

Okay, so I've never been kissed.

And the last place I want to experience my first is in front of thousands of people.

Okay, maybe not thousands, but still. Even just one other person would be bad enough—and, oh gosh—*I'm getting crinkly just thinking about it*—but why does my *first* have to be in front of someone like Diggs? I mean, is he going to coach us? Direct? Provide tips?

Agh!!! I can't stand it!

What is a kiss doing in a middle-school play? Isn't that like PG-13 material?

Okay, so I'm older than thirteen—but that doesn't mean I'm ready and willing to act like it all the time.

I take the script from my bedside table, flip to the final pages.

Maybe Diggs will allow a few changes. What's the difference if the spell is broken with a kiss on the lips, or a kiss on the cheek? Or the hand? A kiss is a kiss, right? When Prince Bastian is holding me in his arms, we could do a kiss on the cheek. That wouldn't be so bad.

I drop the script in my lap.

Why am I even thinking I'll make it to the final scene?

This whole play is going to be a disaster, with or without the kiss. *I'm Nelle.* And it's not going to be good.

Plus, if I couldn't get Diggs to change his mind about the roles, he's not going to change anything about *this*.

I reach up and swat a red balloon left over from the science fair. It dips down and skims my white rug, where it slows into a lame spin. I'm startled when Wren appears behind it.

"Aw," she says, with a tip of her head. She slaps her hands through the balloon. "Y' look sorrier than the cat who ate the pig. What's wrong with ye?"

I look at her, don't say anything and roll over, pretending to read.

Wren slips in front of me, hovering on her knees. Her long tufts of hair fall through my arms. "They won't be having ye in the play now, will they?"

She reads the slight arch of my brow, darts back in surprise. "Well, no glory be to God! Yer in?"

I nod.

"How did y' be getting to do that?"

I raise my hands in frustration. "Because you got me the lead?"

This truly is more of a question, than a statement. I still can't believe it.

Wren's mouth drops open in bewilderment. Her face changes from horror to delight. "Well, isn't that the news that makes me day!"

"Hardly."

"Well, it means I did ye a good job. I didn't totally flub it up for ye."

"Wren... I wasn't supposed to get a part."

She rolls her shoulders to brush off her excitement, leans back, sinking a little into the wall. "Tell the teacher you can't, then."

"Tried. Didn't work."

"Oh...." Wren kneads her hands at her thighs. "Well, there's got to be something good to be got. Who'll be the prince?"

As if she doesn't know.

"That boy, Duey? The one we tried out with?"

She squeals before I even get a chance to reply.

"Awww. Don't tell me there isn't a wee bit of gladness in ye! Acting in a fairytale with a boy as good-looking as Heaven is reason enough to turn a jig through the floor!"

"Maybe for you. But just so you know, by today's standards, Duey is not all that good-looking."

Wren crosses her arms, spins a circle in the middle of the room. "That'd be news to my ears. And yers, too, if they didn't know ye was saying it. If they hadn't felt what I was feeling when we were reading lines beside him. That wasn't my blood chugging through me heart, blazing me ears red with heat."

"I'm sure you had something to do with it."

She juts her nose up in defiance. "Kept ye on yer feet, I did. And ye still haven't thanked me for it."

I roll my eyes, pull a face. "Thanks."

Wren drops to a silent heap on the floor, tucks her knees in under her long, drifty skirt. "Yer telling me yer not the least bit excited?"

When I don't answer, she looks away. "I'd die at the chance to play the likes of Nelle, to be meeting the prince of me dreams—"

"Well, that makes one of us."

"How can you be turning on luck as good as gold?" She shakes her head, slaps her hands through the floor, although not intentionally. After a moment, her eyes go even more cloudy. "Goll, Myr, how can ye not like it? Being up there on that stage... for the first time in me life... it was amazing! And *I could read!* With yer help, with yer mind—I could read again!"

"What do you mean?"

"Yer brains... with my brains... they didn't go forgetting, just because I was stepping in."

Wren shakes her head, courses her hands over her throat. "Those words were singing themselves out of me mouth.... Twas much better than answering questions in silence about history."

After a moment, Wren ducks her head. I watch as she folds her nightgown in long pleats, moving hand over hand, flattening the faded fabric under her palms.

"Can you feel that?" I blurt. "The wool brushing against your skin?"

She holds a hand up, presses her thumb to her fingertips. "No, not really. It's almost like me mind and me bod are just remembering how it would be, if I were." She shrugs, lifts her eyes to meet mine, then moves to the window, where she fidgets with her hair, her clothes.

I watch her, this ghost of a girl I've known so long. This ghost, who is so full of life, yet, so lost from what it means to be truly living—at least, in this world. And she's certainly not embracing the next. Could she see beyond the window pane? Into the darkness where the stars burned bright? Or, was everything faded into shadow, unable to pass into the fringes of her world?

"I can feel this, though." Taking her hands from the windowsill, Wren cups them together, begins rotating them for an energy ball. "It's weird, but it's the first thing I've ever done on me own—after all these years—that I can feel."

I bring my hands together like hers. "You can feel heat?"

She tips her head, considering. "It's more like how a butterfly would be, flitting against me palms."

I watch, as she rotates her hands around something that seems less real than herself. How is it that someone who doesn't amount to a whisper in the wind can pack so much ferocity for life?

"What do you miss most?" I suddenly ask.

She locks her clouded eyes with mine. "Everything."

Chapter 23

This is a test. This is only a test.

*This is a test of the Emergency Ghost-Possession System.*

*If this had been an actual emergency—as in a real-life, hostile possession—my body, and all its functions would not be working for me at this moment, or ever, perhaps....*

"We have another preparatory exercise to learn for the stage today," Diggs says. "Make yourselves comfortable. On your desk, on your chair, or on the floor, if you prefer. Just make sure you're in a place where I can see you."

Some people move to the floor, but Wren keeps me seated.

We're getting good at this—Wren and me—in working things out with drama.

Every morning, we wake up, go to school, sit at my desk, and then, Wren takes over like she's supposed to.

And everyday, when Diggs takes attendance, he doesn't know that technically, I'm not here—at least, not sitting in my own skin. Which is great. It truly amounts to one hundred percent *me-time*.

I don't have to deal with Brittley's hostile looks. I don't have to deal with the smell of Jordan Droone's feet, when he pumps up his aerator sneakers—*swish, swish, swish*—to air out his sweaty feet. I don't have to deal with the embarrassment that washes over me when I read my lines.

Nope. I don't have to deal with any of that. Smell and touch don't make it to my side of the world. Wherever my side is…. I haven't quite found the boundaries.

But I've laid plenty of boundaries for Wren. The first being, *stay in the back row*. If she's going to be me, then she's going to do it with as little attention as possible. That means, no talking, unless spoken to. No silly mannerisms from the 18th century, unless they're needed for rehearsal (*NOT liking that detail*). No kid-like goof-ups—which, so far, haven't been a problem. After three hundred years, even a twelve-year-old ghost can act mature. Kind of. When she wants to.

"It's good to hear your stage voices so early in the day," Diggs says, "but let's put them away, so we can begin."

For a drama teacher, Diggs is turning out to be kind of cool, although he'd be a whole lot cooler, if he'd stop calling my mom. Not that he's calling the house. He's calling her cell phone, which makes it even more annoying with the way she ducks out of the room.

She's never done that—step out to take a call. And she's never laughed so much on the phone, either, which is a change, so I know they're not talking about death and burials. But what makes him so funny?

"Today, we're going to be learning about what may be the oldest word in human language. Or, at least what some say is linked to the origins of the universe and its infinite space. What do you think of that?"

No one says anything.

"Repeat after me. 'Ohhhmmmmm.'"

Some kids giggle, including Wren, because *yeah*, that's funny, even if it sounds dorky.

Diggs holds up a hand. "This is serious, kids. Give it a try. There's a good reason we're doing this."

He starts humming. This time, most of the students join him. "Ohhhmmmm!"

The ohms go up and down, which he directs like a music conductor.

"Can you feel that vibration?" Diggs asks.

"The whole class feels like it's vibrating," Duey replies. He's sitting two rows over, between Cam and another kid named Warren Sims.

"That's right. It does. But can you feel it inside you, as well?"

Brittley nods from her seat in the front row. "It kind of tickles. Right here." She points to the center of her chest.

Diggs nods, pushes himself off the desk, and walks down the center aisle. "Scientists study the feeling of peace that this word, ohm, can bring." Pausing, he looks to opposite sides of the room. "Do some of you feel more calm as you say it?

"Well, keep saying it, please."

"Ohhhmmmmm."

A curt laugh erupts from my throat. "Sounds more like the tune the poor cow died of!"

Cass titters from her desk.

I slap my hand over my mouth. *Quiet!*

Diggs shoots me a glance, before returning to the front of the room. "This word, *Ohm,* may be the oldest word in the human language. But more than that, as drama students, it's *imperative* that you learn how to harness the inner feeling of peace it conveys.

"Because harnessing that peace, learning to clear your head of what makes you *you*, will help you tap into your character. It will help you learn what makes that character real. And, if you use it before your performances, it can help quiet the unavoidable, last-minute jitters." He circles his hands up. "Say it with me! Ohhhmmmmm."

"Ohhhmmmmm!"

"I'd like you to add this to your mental tool box. File it with your Veee's, your Vaah's, and your Voh's."

Wren clears my throat. "And those be the ones that the giant died of! When he fell off the stalk after wee little Jack."

Cass gives me weird look. "That's fee, fi, fo, fum. Not veee, vaah, voh."

Duey laughs. "Vee-vah the cow!"

It takes barely a second for Cam to translate Duey's attempt at Latin. "Long live the cow?"

"Yeah, viva the cow," Duey replies. He laughs, leans forward to look across the aisle at Wren (a.k.a., me). "Nice."

Wren shoots him a flirty wink.

Thankfully, we have a ringleader. Diggs gives a piercing whistle to quiet all the fees and fahs and vahs and voohs "I think this calls for a homework assignment!"

The entire class groans. Everyone that is, but Wren. She sits me up with an eager jolt.

"Yes, a homework assignment," he repeats. "On words that bring inner peace. Words that are known as *mantras*. One page, typed, double-spaced. Due next Tuesday. That should give you more than enough time to do it over the weekend.

"And!" Mr. Diggs adds over the grumbles that follow. "To give you a hint on where to start, you may want to look into methods of meditation." He grins at the unrest rising around him. "Now, take out your scripts."

Cass leans toward me, as she digs into her backpack. "Would you like me to kill you now, or later?"

"Hate to tell you," I mutter, pushing Wren out. "I'm already half-way there."

Chapter 24

"Hold still." Mom tugs me back on the stool, where we can both watch the fitting in the bathroom mirror. "Let me pin this horn in place."

"I thought female goats didn't have horns." I reach back to scratch an itch between my shoulder blades, but I can't press through the fur of the costume.

"They do. I checked." She pauses to scratch my back. "Mountain goats have curved horns, both the males and females."

"Do they have to be so big?" I swat the yellow horn curling on the side of my head. It barely moves, given that it's as thick as my fist.

Mom presses her lips around a pin, eyes me in the mirror, then takes the pin from her mouth. "The horns are fine. If you ask me, this mask is better than what was shipped by that company. I can always go back to that one, if you want."

I swivel my head, not agreeing either way.

Mom stands back to read my expression; then lets out a defeated sigh, when she can't. "Since you've been cursed close to one hundred years, Myri, I'd think you'd have to look it, just a little."

I'd rather not have to be in the play and look like anything at all. But she and I have had that conversation, and we both know there's no getting out of it. And even though I'm no longer tied to the play in a physical sense (thanks to Wren), emotionally, when I stop and think about it, I still get completely messed up.

Frustrated by my silence, Mom comes round to face me. "Look, Myri, I've got less than two weeks to work with here, and twenty other costumes that need to be touched up and finished—for kids I don't live with, so I'd appreciate it, if you'd cut me a little slack. I'm doing what I can to help make this play good. Maybe you need to do the same. Don't you have lines to practice?"

I pull the mask off my head, let it drop to the counter. "Yep, and for your information, I've been more than taking care of it."

When I push open the door to Gram's bedroom, I expect to find her reading a book on her bed—something she usually does before her afternoon nap. Instead, I find the room darkened, the shades drawn, and all the furniture—the bed, the coffee table, the odds and ends—pushed back against the walls to make space for a central card table draped with a satin red cloth.

Gram and Mrs. Gertestky are sitting at it, facing each other, their palms pressed flat on the table between them. It's hard to tell if the ghost, who is sitting in his chair, even notices the three white tea candles burning in front of him.

Seeing me hesitate, Gram beckons me in. I gather a quick glance of my surroundings, before closing the door. As far as I can tell, the only light in the room is coming from those tiny candles.

My eyes squint, before adjusting to the darkness. "What's going on?"

"A séance. We're trying to reach him," Mrs. Gertestky says, giving the ghost a nod.

"With a cup of tea?" My eyes settle on the three white cups near the candles.

Gram half-laughs, pulls me into her with a hug. "No, no. We're using the cups to read his fortune— his future—or, at least, what his future was supposed to be. You see, he keeps checking his pocket-watch, so he must have been wanting to go somewhere or meet someone before he died."

"But wasn't his future cut short? That meeting, or whatever it was, was missed?"

"Yes, but he certainly still believes he has one," Gram says. "And that may be enough to influence the cups."

Mrs. Gertestky pats the table, locks eyes with Gram. "But if he never responds to anything other than that watch, he may be forever stuck."

I distract my mind from that possibility by leaning forward to peer into the cups, expecting to see brown liquid, or the flecks of black tea leaves ringing the bottom, but they're empty.

"Here," Mrs. Gertestky says, jingling an armful of bracelets. She taps the table with a curled finger. "Take a seat next to your grandmother. I'll show you."

She touches her turban, taps the table again, insisting I sit.

I know I'm not getting out of the room until I do, so I get the vanity stool from Gram's dresser. Gram brushes her shoulders with mine, as I sit. My stomach tumbles into a fit of fluttering. I've never seen a fortune told. I didn't know Mrs. Gertestky did this.

She circles her hands above the center of the table, and as if casting a spell, mutters some strange words. After a moment, she carefully inverts each cup over each candle. The room grows dim, as their light is covered and extinguished. A candle I hadn't noticed burning on the bookshelf behind us intensifies the shadows on the walls, shielding Mrs. Gertestky's face in darkness.

Her words are brisk. "Each cup before you now holds heat and fire—elements of human desire." She looks across the table at me, her green-gray eyes in shadow. "Myri, I ask you... concentrate on who you are. Where you want to be... ten days, five months, six years from now—"

"Wait, you're reading *my* fortune? I thought this was for Old Top Hat." I tip my head at the transparent dude sitting next to me.

"No. To show you, I'll do yours. His can come later. Now, think about you. Myri Anna Monaco. That is all we will focus on. Time does not matter. Space does not matter. Let the cups fill with a message for you. To do so, ask the candles laying underneath the cups a question. The one you choose will hold your answer."

I let out a quick huff, reach across the table.

Mrs. Gertestky shoots her arm out, stops my hand as it hovers over the cup that is closest to me. "*Choose wisely*, Myri. Choose with intent. Even fate can read apathy. If you do this, and you don't care?" She tsks. "It can affect your future in a bad way."

I meet her eyes. "We're talking about a tea cup."

"No, a *gateway*. A glimpse at the future. The tea cup may be a vessel, but make no mistake, it can hold all that's important to you."

I shoot a look at Gram, thinking, yeah, right. This is the cup I drank hot chocolate from this morning. But I withdraw my hand and close my eyes, anyway.

*I do need something good to happen.* I really do.

When I take in a shaky breath, my head swims.

According to Mrs. Gertestky, if I'm going to get something good, then I need to give this whole question-and-answer-thing about my future my best effort.

Tipping my head to one side, I ask the candle a question and focus on what I want.

Nothing out of the ordinary happens. The candle behind us doesn't flicker. The table doesn't shake. A crow doesn't rap at the window.

I reach for the nearest cup again, set my hand on it, when suddenly, a thought hits me. *Is this really the cup I want?* If one of these cups does hold answers about my future, don't I want to know what they are?

Letting go of the first cup I chose, I quickly upright the other I'm drawn to. The one in the middle.

A strong scent of sandalwood and musk seeps through the air from the extinguished candle that was sitting underneath. Dipping into the up-righted cup with her fingertips, Mrs. Gertestky pulls her arm up in a long, graceful arch. Smoke follows her fingers, swirling like a delicate white ribbon, before setting on a path toward the ceiling.

With a circle of her hand, Mrs. Gertestky disentangles herself from the smoke's journey and sits back in her chair.

The trail of smoke curls and unfurls in small, gentle waves. Some ribbons, thinning into thread-like strands, hover close to the table and fold back into the cup. For a moment, I'm almost disappointed that the connection between the smoke in the cup and the smoke dancing a ballet at the ceiling will be severed.

Yet, swirls of smoke re-emerge, fanning their way around the cup's rim, as if pulled by an invisible force, before spilling onto the table.

Mrs. Gertestky's gaze moves toward the cup I had originally meant to tip. The cup on the left. The inverted rim is propped at an angle on the edge of the candle sitting underneath. In my haste, I'd not reset it to lie flat, and now a thin stream of smoke is escaping—curling out in a slithering mass toward the cup I chose.

Mrs. Gertestky's eyes widen, then narrow, as the two bodies of smoke merge, then fan out, before slowly fading away. Concern fills her face. "It's a warning," she says.

Gram takes in a worried breath. "What does that mean?"

Mrs. Gertestky's eyes cloud, as she raises them to meet mine. "It means, stay straight on the paths you follow, Myri. Don't be pulled from your future by another." Her brow furrows at the base of her turban. "The cups are telling you, stay straight on the paths you follow."

Chapter 25

For the rest of the weekend, my paths brought me through a list of chores that I had to finish on Saturday and my lovely drama assignment, which took up most of Sunday. (I'm not the world's fastest typist.)

Plus, it was hard to come up with a whole page of things to say about *Hamsa* (a meditation word that means, Who am I?) and *Soham* (another meditation word that means, I am that), until I pretended I was Diggs.

Sick and wrong, I know. But it worked.

Pretending to be Diggs was the only way I could fill my paper with long, flowing, smart-sounding sentences. I couldn't believe how easy it was to write the assignment, once I got into the groove. It was so easy, in fact, that I think pretending to be other people is a good thing. There's so much that can done!

Which is why I was almost giddy to be back in school this morning. Or, not back in school—at least when it comes to drama club. Wren's been doing a great job pretending to be me. So good, that most of the time it feels like I'm not there.

English class is another story, however. And my stomach has been letting me and everyone else know that I'd appreciate being let out early for lunch.

Roz may be partly to blame. She's taking a quiz in *Teen Life*, trying to discover which cookie her personality resembles most. Based on where her finger is pointed on the page, it looks like she's heading in the direction of either a gingersnap or a cocoa crinkle. Which, of course, has absolutely nothing to do with what Miss Augustus is talking about.

"In the art of persuasion," she's saying, "you need to be convincing, whether you believe in what you're saying or not. It's critical, really. You'll need to keep that in mind when you work on your next set of essays. In them, you'll demonstrate your understanding of persuasion."

Samantha Wheeler raises her hand, grinning. "Persuasion is like lying then? We have permission to lie in our essays? I'm not sure if my parents will like that."

Miss Augustus starts to reply, then lets her arms dangle by her side. This is her first job out of college, and we tend to frustrate her with these types of questions. Some kids even make a sport of it—seeing how many times they can get her to let out a deep breath, rub her forehead in frustration, cry—she's cried twice.

But today, Miss Augustus is saved by the bell, and so are we, since she doesn't have time to finish going over the assignment.

Roz grins up at me, as I sit on the corner of her desk. "Ready?"

"I'm a gingersnap," she says. "And you're a sugar cookie. I did your quiz for you."

"That seems to be the new trend."

Roz steps with me into the hall. "So... I've been meaning to ask.... How's drama?"

I shrug. "It's going all right."

"And Wren? She's okay with everything?"

"Yep. We're getting along."

"How about Duey?"

"What is this? Twenty questions?"

"Ye-ahh. Has he talked about me lately?"

Crap. If I were to be honest, I'd have to say no.

"Well, I know he's not interested in Brittley, like you thought he would be." I figure that's one thing she'll be happy to hear. "Even though they're in the play together, it's not happening."

"It's not?" Roz pauses mid-step, as her look of confusion spills into delight at the possibilities she thinks are opening before her. "Really? Are you sure?"

I suck in my lips until they smack apart. "Yep. That's what it looks like, but it's hard to tell. All we've been doing in class and at rehearsals is read the play aloud, over and over, so that in the event of a disaster—like, someone forgetting their lines, or throwing up, or getting abducted by aliens—the show can go on, because someone will be able to step in. We're all understudies for everyone else."

"Oh."

"So, I haven't really talked to him, or seen him all that much."

"You're in a play with him," she says, her voice going flat.

"Well, yeah, but that doesn't mean we talk about his life."

She doesn't say anything, and that's okay. Everything I've said is true. I mean, he definitely doesn't seem to be going out with Brittley, anymore—she must have reeled in that newsflash before it got around. Typically, stuff like that— who's going with whom, and who's dumping whom— spreads like wildfire before it even happens.

And Duey only *hinted* at the fact he would be okay with going out with me. Nothing more was said on that issue to clarify whether he thinks he's my boyfriend. And even though he does seem to hanging closer to me—talking to me after class and rehearsal—technically, when it comes to time spent in drama, he's not himself. He's Prince Bastian. And I'm *really* not myself. I'm Wren, who's playing me, who's playing Nelle. Which is tricky, now that I think of it.

Duey did say, "See you at rehearsal," to me this morning, after sliding a Twix bar in my pocket. But that's a given (the what-he-said-part, not the Twix part). It's something he'd say to anyone in the play.

But it would have been better if he'd said, "Say hi to Roz for me," or, "Tell Roz to come by rehearsal."

...I'm working on that. And if that means I have to keep playing up to the 'that'd-be-more-than-okay' hypothetical-girlfriend-idea, so that Brittley can't be his real-girlfriend, then so be it. It's all being done so that good things can happen between Roz and Duey.

Eventually.

The sooner the better, actually.

Because now that Roz is asking about him again, this whole deal is starting to make me nervous.

So nervous in fact, that for the first part of rehearsal tonight, I'm going to be me. That way, I can talk all about Roz to Duey. Remind him of all the good qualities he couldn't resist in the past. Then I can have better answers for Roz's questions. Answers she wants to hear.

"Well, tell him I said, 'hi,'" she says, backing down the hall toward her Spanish class.

"I will."

Now I just have to get him to do the same.

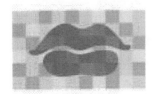

## Chapter 26

"We have a problem." I push the script across the kitchen table toward Wren.

She drops her hands from an energy ball, floats higher in her chair to look.

"What'll be eating y' now?"

"The kiss. At the end. It can't be done."

Her head pulls back. "Sure it can. It's how he breaks me spell."

"Well, yes. But that's not what I mean. *You* can't kiss him. It has to be me. It didn't occur to me until today."

Wren's mouth drops. "But that's the best part! I don't want to be stepping out for that."

"I don't want you to step out for it, either, but you have to. It's too close of a touch. If you kiss, he might see you."

"He won't see me. How can he see me when it's yer bod that I'm setting in?"

"He might see double. And that would be weird. He could totally freak. Which wouldn't be good for me, you, or the play. And if it happened in rehearsal, we wouldn't be able to do what we do anymore. *You* won't be able to do what you do anymore. And Duey might get all revved up about ghosts in the theater again."

Wren goes silent. She knows I'm right. Touches, bumps on the arm—she and Roz had already figured out those were fine when they did the history test. But a kiss? That's much more. That could be like walking through a ghost on any given night—when, with the chill, the instant sight, you suddenly realize you're not alone. And we needed Duey to think that throughout the play, I was up there on that stage alone.

## Chapter 27

"Girls. Boys. Attention, please. Thank you. I know we haven't gotten through all of Act One today, and I know we are running short on time, but I'd like to run through the final scenes in Act Two."

Crap. The scene Wren can't do.

I look around at the theater. Where is she? She said she'd be back in a minute, but that was five minutes ago. Sure, she can't do the scene, but I don't want her showing up in the middle of it, thinking she needs to help me, and jump in at the worst possible moment.

"The reason is," Diggs continues, holding his hands in the air until everyone stops talking. "The reason is that *this is the climax* of our story. This is what we are all working toward. This is where our characters are *most alive*. This is where their dreams *are either made*, or shattered. And as actors, as *thorough actors*, we need to understand what attaining or losing those dreams means."

Well. I know what it means to me. It means I've got to lie down on this stage on my own and look dead, which I'm hoping will not be all that hard.

"Nelle's dream is different from Prince Bastian's dream," Diggs continues, "which is different from Witch Ekatera's, which is different from King Wester's, and even those of the soldiers. We have to understand what each one of us is working toward."

I'm working toward not being kissed. At least, that's what I'd like to work toward. If I weren't going to be kissed, then Wren could be Nelle through the whole play.

Diggs spins from the table at the side of the stage with his script binder in hand. "If you could all take your places.... Narrator. Nelle. Soldiers One, Two, Three. Prince Bastian.... We're in the scene after Witch Ekatera, in a fit of jealousy, has just ordered her soldiers to go to the bakery to do our poor heroine in."

He looks over at Londyn, who is hesitating at stage-right. "Yes, Londyn, that's fine, right there. Pretend we have an audience." He spins his hands forward, gesturing her to start speaking in her role as narrator, when Brittley jumps up at the back of the stage, swinging her blue-and-white-striped binder from her hip.

Her shirt is also blue. But her pants—*we're talking big diet RISK here*—are khaki. She strides to the front of the stage. "So, you don't need me?"

"No." Diggs steps down to his seat at stage-left.

"Are you sure?"

"Yes. This is the start of scene five, Act two. Not the end of scene four."

Londyn is waiting by the curtain. He gives her a nod. "Whenever you're ready. Places, everyone!"

I grab a brown plastic tray and stand near the right side of the stage, wishing that the counters for the bakery scene were set up. At least I'd have something to stand behind, instead of looking like a fool in the middle of nothing. Everyone else gets to wait for their cues behind the curtains.

Londyn clears her throat. "The soldiers set out at once. It was easy to find the bakery. As her new friendship with Prince Bastian had blossomed, so had Nelle's passion for baking. The aromas of a thousand different dishes drew the soldiers to the stoves where she labored.

"But even the promise of baklavas and Danishes, mincemeats and stews could not soften the savagery of their mission."

With her introduction to the scene finished, Londyn nods with a smile and steps aside. Soldier One, played by a boy named Nate Bilyard, emerges from the eaves.

"There she is!" he says, thrusting a finger toward me. "The monster with the head of a goat!"

Yes, one of my better qualities. Thank God I'm not wearing the mask now.

Although it suddenly occurs to me. Maybe I should be? It might help.

Soldier Two steps forward and stamps his foot. "The beast with the flesh of a snake!"

Even more lovely.

Soldier Three raises his arm as if to swing a sword. "The creature with the hump of a camel! Surround her!"

I drop my tray and run to the back of the stage where I pretend to climb stairs—which I'm told will be set up tomorrow. I let out a cry for, "help!" but at the moment, I can't tell if that's just me reacting out of fear, or if it's something that's really a part of the play. I can't remember. But with the soldiers in quick pursuit, waving their bows and arrows, it really does feel like I'm in trouble. As they take aim, I do my best to hide behind a wood bench.

"Hold your fire!" Duey runs to the center of the stage.

But the arrow from Soldier Three flies and it hits... (imagination working), and I get to play dead. (Finally!)

With my heart beating its way out of my chest, with concrete spilling into my lungs, pretending to be dead is a welcome experience.

"You will pay for your treason at the gallows!" Duey yells.

The soldiers retreat, whispering amongst themselves, as Duey kneels, slipping his arm under my neck, making my pulse quicken even more.

"Forgive me, my Lady, I have failed." He looks at me as if I'm the sorriest thing he's ever seen, which I hope is all part of the act.

My eyes dart from his, as I swallow, "There you are my silly friend, my silly prince, calling *me*—a woman who's no more than a goat—*a lady.*"

Diggs clears his throat. "Louder, please! Even with a microphone, no one will be able to hear you. I know you're dying, *I know*, but you've still got to speak your lines loudly and clearly, as you've always done. Remember, however, there is a balance. While I want you to be loud, you still need to make your imminent death believable to the audience."

I huff. *My imminent death.* Like I really know how that feels. Well, fine. If he wants loud, I'll do loud.

"There you are!" I yell. "My silly friend of a prince! Still calling me a lady!" It occurs to me that I said it wrong before. Or, maybe I'm saying it wrong now. I don't know.

A grin spreads across Duey's face, as he tries not to laugh, and matches his voice to my own. "To me, you always will be! My fair lady!"

I can't help but giggle at our yelling at each other. Is this right? Is this how you act when you're dying on a stage?

Okay, it's not right. Diggs is telling us to take it down a notch.

I gasp for a breath, put a hand to my head. "My time is at an end, my dear friend. Who now will see to your pastries?!"

"Focus!" Diggs trumpets from the floor, as we laugh. "I need you to be serious."

Duey moves his hand awkwardly under my head to lift me up.

I know I'm not helping. For someone who's dying, I'm not all that limp and lifeless.

"Slide your arm under her neck and shoulders," Diggs says. "It will look more natural. And, Nelle, relax. You look like you're trying to get away from him.

"Good," Diggs adds, after I let myself fall against Duey's shoulder. "Line, please."

"My dear, Nelle!" Duey says, tilting his head to look me in the eyes—just before I close them. "You can't leave me! I love you! I'd do anything to save your life! I love you!"

I hold my breath, as my stomach goes all queasy hearing those words. This is where he's supposed to kiss me, but he doesn't. He's waiting. Thank God, he's waiting. Because even though the lines were easy, the thought of the kiss isn't.

With a quick peek, I see him looking questioningly at Diggs.

"Yes, yes, the kiss," Diggs says, "which is followed by a brilliant flash of light, and the transformation of Nelle into our new princess Nella Rose." He glances at his watch. "We can skip that for now, seeing as we're out of time."

Pushing myself up on my knees, I roll away from Duey. He jumps up, apparently as relieved as I am. "Uh, Mr. Diggs?" I say. "About that. What if we don't have it?"

"Not have what?"

134

"The kiss."

Disbelief fills his face.

"What if we just leave it at a declaration of love. Save me with that. Couldn't that be enough?"

Brittley strides over to me with her blue and white binder. "How could it be enough? All fairy tales end with a kiss."

"Which is why ours should be different."

"The story is what's different, Myri," Brittley says with a roll of her eyes. "Not the kiss."

"I just don't see why we need it," I retort, copying her attitude with a flip of my head.

I turn to Diggs. After all, he's the one in charge. Not Brittley.

But she keeps talking. "I don't see why you should care, Myri. About the kiss? After all, Duey *is* your boyfriend now, isn't he? At least, that's what he told me. That he's your *boyfriend.*" She brings her hands coyly up in front of her chest, making a heart with her thumbs and fingers for everyone to see. "Why shouldn't you want to kiss him?"

My mouth drops open, as my ears, my head, my chest burn with heat. I let out a little huff, not knowing what to say.

"Why in the world would you want to take out the kiss?" Diggs walks to the edge of the stage to look up at me.

And I thought teachers were supposed to be smart.

Brittley ignores him. "You *are* dating him, aren't you?"

"No." I catch Duey's hurt look of surprise, Brittley's smug look of satisfaction. "I mean, yes. I mean—"

Cass stands up from the seats in the second row, clearly trying to understand what's going on. I throw my hands up in frustration. "What does it matter? That's not the point! I was just thinking about what Mr. Diggs was saying about not being able to hear our lines. If we change the last scene, have Duey declare his love for me, we could fix it." I realize what I've said too late.

"Declare his love *for you?!*" Cam guffaws, coming over from the side of the stage to knock Duey on the arm.

"Nelle, I mean! Have him declare his love for Nelle, while he's yelling at the soldiers! Then we wouldn't have to worry about the balance of our voices, if they're too low, or too high. We could all be angry and yelling at each other. Duey angry at them for shooting me. Me angry at them for shooting me...."

Diggs rubs his forehead, lets out a bewildered laugh. "I don't think so."

"No, wait! This could be perfect," Brittley says, batting her hand in front of her with a sly smile. "Myri may be on to something. Because even though her idea seems stupid, it actually may be a very good one. It ties into what I've been thinking all along!"

She puts her binder down on the floor, so that she can explain with both hands. "Wouldn't it be great if we could change the play? I mean, everyone knows Myri isn't exactly thrilled about stepping in front an audience. It might be better if she could just continue to stay hidden *until the very end.*"

Brittley smiles broadly, opens a hand in my direction. "We really don't need to see her. In fact, if we change the story a little, we don't need to see her at all. We could let her curse be the thing that brings me and Duey together.

"It wouldn't be that hard!" Brittley continues, seeing she has Diggs's attention. "We could make it so that Ekatera is also cursed—that she was cursed at the same time as Nelle, and that they are actually in a competition to see who can get un-cursed first!

"And Nelle could lose because she's too shy about showing her goatsy face to the prince. But in the end, just to show how nice everyone is, Prince Bastian and I—*Ekatera,* I mean—could let her move back to the castle, where she can cook and clean in the kitchen for us. We'd all be living happily ever after.

"And," she adds, throwing me a wicked grin, "*I* wouldn't mind ending the play with a kiss."

Diggs rubs his thumb along a seam in the floor boards of the stage, shakes his head. He opens his mouth to speak, but his chin wavers a moment on his chest. Finally, he looks up at us, first at me, then at Brittley. "You want to rewrite the play?"

Brittley nods enthusiastically. "It wouldn't be all that much work. I can start right now." She picks up her binder, detaches its pen.

Diggs spreads his fingers, clasps his hands, pumps them in front of his chest. "But if we did that, we'd need to create a whole new villain. *Incorporate two villains into our story.* You and this other...." He waves his hand up in the air.

"Witch," Cass finishes for him.

Crap.

I steal a glance in her direction. Her eyes are cold and unflinching. "Maybe they should just switch roles," she adds, her voice hard. "It may be a better fit with the latest developments."

Diggs rolls his eyes to the ceiling, walks a few paces away before spinning back. "I can't believe this. In all my years of directing plays...." His voice trails off. Resting his chin in one palm, he crosses his other arm on his chest. "Although I like the imagination, the desire to be flexible, it can't be done. Not at this point. And it's getting late. Club dismissed."

Everyone scatters. Duey is the first to leave, making me wonder if he's upset, or embarrassed, or both. I shuffle to the side of the stage, grab my bike helmet and backpack from the floor, but before I can go, Diggs calls my name.

"Yeah?"

He rubs a hand across his forehead. "It seemed like you were nervous in tonight's run-through of this scene, Myri, *and that's okay*, but I want you to know that you dropped your accent. I'd like you to bring it back in. It is, after all, what makes Nelle so special."

138

## Chapter 28

"Where'd you disappear to?" I shake the cold from my hair, rip the reflective anklet from my pant leg that I wear for biking, and let it drop to the floor, before focusing, once again, on Wren.

She's lying on my bed, giving her attention to another one of her energy balls. Mom would be proud to know one of us is using our Wolford education.

I march over to the bed, plant my hands on my hips. "Well?"

She lets a long moment pass before finally rubbing her fingers and rolling herself up to sit. "I was with C.J. He was showing me around."

"C.J.?" My heart races.

"Yeah," she continues, not catching the obvious question of 'Who is C.J.?' Instead, she lifts her shoulders to her ears. "Did y' know there's a secret passage at the back of Dressing Room Four?"

"You let one of the drama kids see you?" My voice rises to a shrilly squeak.

A funny look crosses her face, as she waves me off, drifts to my desk, and begins looking at the latest issue of *American Girl* that I'd left lying open.

"No-ooo. Don't be working yerself into a bother. *C.J. is a ghost*. Like me. Yer friend Duey was right. Ardenport Theater does have a wee bit of nightlife after-hours, if ye know what I be saying."

I breathe out a long sigh, before realizing that I'm relieved, of all things, to hear that the theater is haunted.

Wren's face fills with a wistful expression, and I shake my head at the thought of two ghosts dating. *THAT* is not what I want to be thinking about right now.

"Well, you can't be walking off in rehearsal. Even when we're doing the final scene—"

"I missed the kissing scene for tromping around in a secret passage?" She slaps her knee. "Well, push it down a pig's throat. I'm still thinking of a way to do that one!"

"Well, you can't. I couldn't get Diggs to change it. And I don't understand why you'd want to do it, anyway. What do you know about kissing boys?"

"I know enough."

"Yeah, right."

"I do."

I cross my arms, press my weight into my heels.

"Came close, I did. Once." A small smile works across her mouth, before she continues. "And I would've gone through with it, if Sally Mae Robbins hadn't told me Chet had an extra tooth on the top of his mouth that he liked to be using as a tongue-scraper. Turned out that was a lie, because Sally Mae went out kissing him behind the haystacks the next day. Jolly-good friend she turned out to be."

Wren puts her hands to her hips, moves closer. "But the last scene I could do, ye know. Up to the point of the actual kiss, at least. Then I could be stepping out for a breath or two whilst y' do yer business, then step back in, and finish the play like I ought. Unless it be the second night, when it won't be mattering if Duey sees me, because we'll be done."

I shake my head.

Wren turns in a floaty huff, giving her attention back to *American Girl*.

"We need to do the play the way we discussed, Wren. With you doing every scene, but that one. And even when you're not acting in rehearsals, I need you to stick around. There was a huge discussion about the final scene, and you weren't there to hear it. Now if you go talking about something we've already gone over, I'll look dumber than I already do."

I put my hand on the magazine to block her view. "Are you even listening—?" I stop, when I realize what's happened. The magazine page actually slipped out of Wren's hands. *She'd been holding it*, flipping the page, *by herself*.

Her eyes dart back down to the magazine pressed under my palm. She reaches for it, and after a slight hesitation, curls the pages under her fingertips-that-are-not-fingertips. When I pull my hand back, the page lifts under her guidance, and when she lets go, it falls back to the desk.

"How'd you do that?"

Wren slowly shakes her head. "I don't know. I'll be as polly-wogged as y' be over that."

"Wren! That's so cool! You moved something. You actually moved something by yourself!"

She brings her hands up, rotating them slowly in front of her.

I pass my hands through hers, feeling the familiar chill of air. Nothing's changed, at least not there. But when our eyes meet, hers wide with astonishment, I'm reminded that even though she's a ghost, she doesn't know everything. She can't predict the future. And like me, can still be taken by surprise.

## Chapter 29

Monday morning packs me a surprise.

No one is talking to me. Not Roz. Not Cass. Not Elise. Not even Duey, although he did try to smile. But still, as I quickly realized, he isn't the person who's most important to me. It's Roz.

"Just tell me what I did!" I plead, when I manage to grab her by the sleeve before third hour.

She shrugs off my hand, turns to face me in a huff. "It's all over the school, so how could you NOT KNOW?" Her fingers scrunch in mock quotes.

"What are you talking about?"

"Let's see," she says, rolling her eyes to the ceiling. "Let's travel back in time to a little talk we had last week, when you told me Duey wasn't interested in Brittley." She nods, as my mouth drops. "Yeah, I guess that wasn't an out-and-out lie. Only technically, your lack of additional information was. That it's YOU he's actually interested in. You're dating. Or were dating. People are taking bets to see which side wins out."

"Dating? We see each other at rehearsals."

"Close enough. Especially since that's what he's calling it."

"What HE's calling it? Look, you don't understand. That isn't what I planned."

"Yeah, right. Just like you didn't plan to land the leading role with him. If I didn't know better, I'd think you had this whole thing worked out from the beginning."

"I didn't!"

She holds up a hand at my words, shuts her eyes tight. "Let me ask you this," she says, her voice hissed. "Just how much of you is really pulling the strings when it comes to Wren? Or, is that all an act, too?"

She stands back, steels me a hard look, juts her chin. "Wren's already told me you're not letting her kiss him in the final scene. Trying to shut out the competition? Even with a ghost?"

"Shhhhh!" I hold my hands out, take a quick look around, before meeting her eyes again. "I'm not! You know I'm not!"

"Yeah, right. Why don't you save your arguments for Mrs. Augustus's essay on persuasion. I bet it'll be your first easy A. But just know that I, for one, am not going to believe a word of it."

All it took was the choice between sitting with the nerds at lunch or sitting with Duey, who was still avoiding any eye contact, to make me realize I can't do it. I can't be me.

And because I happen to live with the best understudy on the planet—i.e., Wren—it didn't take long for me to figure out I can use her full-time.

"You get to live your dream," I say, when I find her reading an old picture book in my navy blue bean bag.

She holds up a finger, her lips moving, as she finishes her sentence. "What dream?"

"Life. School. Learning. Living. All that you ever wanted to keep doing. I want you to be me for the next little while. At least until Saturday, when this play is over."

"I thought you didn't want me in school for the whole day. Especially with the way me mouth is always feeling a need to speak."

I give her a wave of hand, fake half a laugh. "I'm over that. Really. And you do need to be at school this week. I see that now. All sorts of details are being finalized outside class—in the halls, at lunch, in the bus lines after school—" (this is a lie, of course), "and you're missing them because you're not there. I think it'd be better if you were."

She stands, letting the book which she'd been holding fall to the floor. I'm still blown away that she can manage that. To anyone else who couldn't see her, that book would have been floating.

"Are ye sure?" she says, her voice beginning to gush with excitement. "Ye won't be teasing me now. I thought ye might be leaning the other way. Of not having me be in the play *at all*, seeing as y' were getting used to doing that one scene on yer own."

"No, I'm not teasing you. I want you to be me for the whole day. Every day. This whole week."

She scoffs like she doesn't believe me. "Why would y' be having me do that?"

"Why not? It's only a few days. Till the play's done. It's like Mom said, you can learn something. I already know most of it, anyway. A week away on my end won't hurt. Besides, you want to be there more than I do, anyhow. So, what do you say?"

I wait, holding my breath, thinking I can fill her in on the minor details later—of my needing new friends, a new lunch table, a new morning locker routine....

Knowing Wren, those details won't phase her. She's witty enough, brave enough, to go out and forge a whole, new social network.

After a moment she comes over and extends her arm, holding up her palm in front of me. I place mine across hers. It's only a matter of seconds before the heat of mine mixes with the chill of hers, bridging the gap in the middle.

"Till death be tearing us apart," she says with a giggle.

It's the first time I've heard her joke about not being alive.

Maybe that's a good thing. Maybe she's finally come to accept where she belongs—or, where she is—and ultimately—although I doubt we'll ever lose her—where she has yet to go.

I muster the energy to return her smile, meet the dark recesses of her eyes. This deal is supposed to be a good thing. To help Wren help me, and not just because I've been dumped by my friends.

"Till death do us part," I say.

 Chapter 30

The ground rules are this—
1. Don't say anything stupid.
2. Avoid Roz, Cass, and Elise. Roz would know Wren in a heartbeat, and I'm not sure what she'd do if she found out I'm not "all there."
3. If anyone asks what's up with the accent (which they have), Wren is to say she's staying in character to practice for the play. This, as it turns out, has already earned me brownie points from Diggs, who used me as an example for the class.
4. Do my school work. That's right. If she's in class, she can do the work. As payback for all this "living again."

## Chapter 31

I didn't know life could be this great.

Okay—so I'm not entirely living it on my own. I'm getting a whole lot of help from Wren, but still. This whole body possession project has gone much better than I expected.

For one thing, I've got a new set of friends. Sure, I have nothing in common with them, and their wardrobes seem to be limited to various shades of gray and tan, which I suspect may have something to do with their interest in history, but at least I'm not roaming the halls and lunch room alone, and at least I don't have to really talk with them. Wren does that, and they love her for it, especially since she knows *so much* about all things historic. They got all sorts of tips for their history reports, which were due… yesterday….

I have no idea what Wren did for mine….

Not that it matters. She said she'd take care of it, so I have to believe she did. I just wonder how I missed an entire class.

Oh, well. When will I ever get another chance to get credit for a class presentation I didn't do?

Never.

Which leads to the other thing that's turned out so great. I love not being me. No more skin blushing red, no more stuttering like a fool in front of a class, no more breaking out into a sweat when I think about Duey.

In La-La Land I don't have to feel anything, be anything, or do anything to get by. And time goes by so quickly. It's almost as if time stands still for me, while it ticks by for the rest of the world, which makes being here—floating nowhere—so easy.

But even Wren has her limits, and there's only so much of me she can stand, which is obvious when she suddenly decides to slip out, like now, when we're supposed to be heading for the bus.

"See y' later, now!" she says, making me feel like she's literally pulled a rug out from under my feet. I fight to keep my balance, as she slides off toward the far corner of the school yard. It's a good thing I decided to check up on her. She might have left me here for nothing but a bag of bones.

"Where are you going?" I call out, knowing that with the clamor of kids anxious to find their rides home, I'll look like I could be talking to anybody.

"The theater. C.J. will be waiting for me!"

I run after her, not caring if I have audience. I probably just look like a girl running, only not after anything that anyone (aside from Roz) can see.

"Are you going to stay there until rehearsal tonight? Or, are you coming home first?"

"I'll be staying. But ye'll be wanting to pull yer own strings. Yer mother is bringing the costumes for final fitting and dress rehearsal. And since she's not supposed to know about our little arrangement, I don't think ye'll be wanting me around."

"Oh." I had no clue about the costumes. (Must be another one of those moments I was taking a time-out.)

With an echoing, joyful, "Goodbye-now!" Wren dashes off, fading into the field like a dandelion seed blown on the wind.

Standing there, feeling the weight of my own skin, I'm envious of her position—her ability to slip from one life to the next, enjoying the best moments that both worlds have to offer, without having to live through the gut-wrenching details.

Chapter 32

I'm parking my bike outside Ardenport Community Theater, having found the energy to bring myself to this last rehearsal, when Roz appears. Only she doesn't *appear-appear* out of thin air, the way Wren does. She just steps up to me from around the corner.

I skitter back, catching my balance on the seat of my bike, before leaning forward to fumble with the lock. Nerves, laced with panic, boil in my gut, as I clamp the chain closed. Letting my fingers brush the seat, I give Roz a fake smile to show I'm not bothered.

"One hundred and forty-seven loin-cloths?"

That's what she says. I'm not sure how to respond.

Judging by the tone of her voice and the look on her face, I think I'm supposed to know what she's talking about.

Roz blocks my path, as I step toward the doors. "Admit it," she says, taking my arm.

"Admit what?" It occurs to me that I'm a horrible understudy for being, of all things, me.

"Admit you've been letting Wren take over the past week."

I swing my backpack to my other shoulder, shift the weight in my feet.

"Well?"

"Well, I haven't."

"Really? Then explain the loin cloths."

I brush my fingers through my hair, roll my eyes in frustration. "Explain *what* about what loin cloths? I have no idea what you're talking about."

"Exactly," Roz says. She puts her hands on her hips, takes a step closer. "You've been cutting school. *This whole time.* You've been sending Wren in your place."

"Nope."

Roz shakes her head. "There's no way you'd get up in history *by yourself* and go on and on about the history of underwear."

My mouth drops. Roz's presses into an affirmative line.

"Mr. Scanlin had to cut you off. Well, *not you. Wren.* The only girl between us who knows what people wore down to the tiniest details before underwear was even invented. And a girl who probably has connections to those who might know how many loin cloths King Tutankhamen was actually buried with in Egypt."

"One hundred and forty-seven?"

She nods.

I let out a breath of defeat. "When did that happen?"

"Yesterday. Funny you don't know."

"Well, I know now." I make a move to get past her, but she blocks my path again.

"Don't you think that's going a bit far?"

"No. And why would you care? It's not like you and I have been talking."

"Me and her, you mean."

"It's still me."

"Is it?"

"Close enough." I stretch the cricks in both sides of my neck, let out a breath. "I'm just giving Wren a chance to do something she never did."

Roz crosses her arms, gives me a raised-eyebrow look.

"And giving myself a vacation."

Roz throws her hands up, before slapping them down to her thighs. "I thought Wren was just supposed to get you through auditions. I guess I can understand why you'd let it go further into helping with the whole play. But Myri. Your whole life? You're giving that away, too?"

"I'm not giving away my life."

"Oh, really." Her voice goes flat.

"Not permanently, anyway."

"Even if it's just temporary, it's not good. She's not you, Myri. Not even close."

"So?"

Her eyes go wide. "So?" she says, mocking me. She changes course. "What about Duey?"

I shrug.

"You're letting her get him, too, you know."

This gets my attention. I can't help it. My ears tingle, my heart pounds. I didn't realize he and I were still talking all that much.

"Who does he really know, Myri?" Roz says, studying me with a serious gaze. "The fun girl who can be the best friend in the world, or Wren, the poor Irish understudy."

My stomach flip-flops, as what she's said sinks in. I squirm at the words hanging between us.

"What do you mean, *best friend?*"

Roz turns red, shuffles her feet.

"I thought you didn't want me to be with him. And you certainly haven't wanted me to be *your friend.*"

"I don't... I mean...." She takes a breath. "Look, we're just friends—Duey and I—I know that. But the other day, I realized I like it better being friends with you." She runs her fingers through her dark hair, which I see she's cut into long layers and added more highlights. She lets out another breath. Her arms drop to her sides. "Boys can be such a hassle. Why should we even bother?"

I let out a half-laugh. "Yeah, Duey's a dork. A *nice* dork," I clarify. "He hadn't even asked Brittley out.... Or me."

"I know. I heard."

"You did?"

She nods. "He told me."

"It wasn't supposed to become real, you know? I was trying to point out his stupidity. Not be played into it."

"I know."

"I was only trying to get him to like you again. That was my plan."

She lets out a huff, looks away. "I'm sorry I didn't give you a chance to explain."

"So, you know we're not really going out?"

Roz tips her head. "I wouldn't go so far as to think that. He really likes you."

"He does?" My heart quickens.

She nods. "At least he thinks he likes you. But right now, with the way things are, the only person he's been talking to is Wren. That's got to be a bit hard for him to follow. I know it's hard for me."

My face goes hot, as Roz kicks a pebble, lets her eyes meet mine. "She's not good at being you, Myri. And she's got you a whole new set of friends; and they don't even know the difference." She half-laughs. "Some friends."

My throat clamps so tight, I barely manage a whisper. "Are you saying you want to be friends again?"

"Yeah," she manages. "If you stop what you're doing with Wren. It's dangerous. It's scary. You should see yourself. It's not you." She shakes her head. "Sorry I keep saying that, but have you even been there at all when she's at school?"

I let out a long breath. "More or less…. Sometimes…. I mean, the more she goes as me, the

156

more she makes these new friends, the more I can't relate, the more it's easier to stay apart from it all."

Roz looks like she's trying to understand. "And where do you stay when you're apart? And how do you do it for so long?"

I shrug. "I don't know. I stay wherever. In bed. In the school hall. In the park, or the backyard. Wherever I want to be. I just think it, and I'm there, like a shadow, only without a body to anchor me. In a way, it's weird, because time almost stands still. It doesn't really feel like Wren's gone as long as she is."

"So, what do you do when she gets back?"

"I don't know. When I see her, I just kind of step in. But...." I pause, as uneasiness washes over me, remembering how it goes. How it's harder and harder to do that.

"But what?"

I let out a long-winded sigh, meet Roz's steady gaze. "I almost need to remember how to breathe, when I get myself back."

Roz kicks one foot, pivots on the other. "That's not good, Myri."

"But once I'm back in, she's not in control," I add, trying to sound optimistic, because to hear myself talk about it out loud scares me.

Roz purses her lips. "Myri... I love Wren, but—"

"You're right. I've got to stop. I've got to stop, before—"

"Before your brain gets turned to mush."

## Chapter 33

Wren's words echo in my head—or, the space of what's left of it.

*Yer sure ye can be doing it? Y' can be Nelle? For the whole play?*

I'd nodded, trying to show confidence.

*Ye won't be wanting me waiting in the wings? Just in case?*

I shook my head. "I'll do the play on my own.... I'll do it. And I'll finish it."

But now, even though I'm saying those words again upon waking. Yelling them, actually. Screaming, as if fires were burning in my blood, those words fall flat, hollow.

I grope for covers I can't grab, push against a bed I can't feel....

Somehow, I'm floating above it all—the covers, my pillow, my bed.

Because my body—
what makes me, *me*—
   is gone.

## Chapter 34

*Wren!!!*

That's all it takes. A thought of her. And immediately, I'm there. Hovering alongside, as she walks toward school with her books—*my books*—pulled close to her chest. My blonde hair flounces across my shoulders, as she walks with that youthful lankiness she hasn't been able to shake. When she pauses to watch a robin that dives across her path, a smile lifts her face. She watches it flit up into the branches hanging over the sidewalk, before walking on.

"Wren," I say, and then again.

Although she's ignoring me, she pauses, just barely, at the second call of her name, making me think I might be able to surprise her with jump back into my body. I try, but it's like meeting a wall. I'm still left hanging in this growing void of space with nothing tangible to grasp onto.

Still, I try again. And again. But it's no use. Somehow, someway, Wren has made my body rock-solid. Rigid. Impermeable to me.

"Wren! Stop!"

This time, she does, turning to face me with my eyes, that are somehow her eyes. With my smile, that is somehow twisting into her smile. My stance, that has somehow shifted into her stance.

"Wren, you can't do this."

Her eyelids flutter in answer.

Panic—churning in waves—settles in the pit of my gut, carving my insides around a gaping hole.

"Sure looks like I can be doing it."

"But you can't! You're the ghost. You're the one who's dead!" I've never said anything like that to her, not with so much anger, so much frustration, or fear.

"Not now, I'm not."

"You just can't take over my life, as if it were yours. I trusted you!"

"Oh, go suck on a babe's bottle, Myri. Yer getting all worked up over nothing, when ye have all the time in the world. A whole lifetime left to be living. And ye say ye can't spare another night for me? I'll be giving yer bod back to ye, sure enough, at the end of the play."

"But you can't be there at the end of the play. You know that."

"After I kiss Duey, I'll be done. Tonight. With the whole play. It won't matter. Ye'll be doing the whole thing on yer own tomorrow."

"It will matter. And you can't kiss him! *You're dead.*" I say it again, hoping those words will sink in.

Instead, we both turn at the unexpected sound of Duey's voice, calling my name.

Running across the school yard with his backpack bouncing from his shoulders, his white-and-blue plaid shirt flaps at his sides over a white skater-tee. Cocking his arm back, he points at the body-formally-known-as-me and lobs the football clutched in his hand. "Myri, catch!"

Wren lets out half a laugh and takes two awkward strides forward. I can almost feel the stretch of my arms as she lifts them up, the pull of my fingers as she spreads them wide.

But of course, it's not me. If it had been, that ball wouldn't have brushed past my fingertips and smacked me in the chest. I wouldn't be spiraling to the ground, laughing, of all things, while the football, bounces around my body, careening this way and that, before coming to a rest at my side.

Oblivious to my wavering presence, Duey jogs past me to Wren, dishing short bursts of laughter between breaths, and I wonder when things got to be so good between us. Last I knew, we were exchanging awkward glances in the halls. How had I missed so much?

He bends to rest his hands on his knees, letting his wavy brown hair fall loose across his forehead. He flips his hair back out of his eyes. "Couldn't you have at least headed it?" he says, referring to my skills on the soccer field, which obviously don't transfer when a ghost is in possession of one's body.

"Since when can you not catch a pancake throw like that?"

"Since the grass be growing at me feet. It's tripping me up being it's so thick and in need of a good trimming."

Duey shakes his head, holds out a hand, and for a moment, jealously twinges in my gut. I wonder what it would feel like to be taking it. How many times has she already felt his fingers threading through mine?

Wren grins, as she takes his hand in her own, curling one side of my mouth; and I drown in another wave of envy.

A tremor takes hold of me, making me feel colder, more disconnected than ever before. I look around—at the trees through my hands, at the grass through my feet, at the one ray of sun that's not obscured by the thickening sky—searching for an answer. What I can possibly do to make things right? To get myself back to the way I was before?

And then I realize, right now? At this moment?

Nothing.

Because if I did the one thing I want to do most—run through him. Through Duey. Fill him with my energy, allow him to see the truth. What would I show?

Nothing but a weak whisper of me.

Chapter 35

It's good to know that in life or death situations, best friends can be counted on.

Although I'm really not sure I want to consider myself hanging anywhere near the edge of death.

Especially when I haven't actually gone through the act of dying.

I had a tough time convincing Roz of that, though. She freaked when she saw me—not that she could at first. I had to hug her to make that happen. Much the way Wren did, I guess, when I was a baby.

Only I don't think I reacted as badly as Roz. But after kicking the wall and banging a few drawers, and sending her mother away who had come to see what was going on in the kitchen, she agreed that after school—or maybe even during, if she could figure out a way to skip out—a trip to see Mrs. Gertestky was in.

## Chapter 36

"The body's grown cold to the spirit it harbored."

These are not the comforting words I'd wanted to hear.

Mrs. Gertestky stares at Roz with her large, green-gray eyes, before circling her arms in front of her. The silver bangles at her wrists jingle and chime until she rests on them on the red tablecloth, curling her wrinkled fingers under her palms.

Roz takes a seat across from her, while I stay near the doorway, wondering if the yellow glow from the candles scattered around the room looks fainter than it should, whether the shadows groping the walls look too dark.

"She's here now?" Mrs. Gertestsky says, lifting her chin slightly.

"Yes," Roz replies.

Mrs. Gertestky extends her arm. "Then let's have her come forward, so we can have a proper. conversation."

Roz shrugs and looks back at me. Mrs. Gertestky opens her palms, raises her hands higher. She wants me to touch them.

Easier said than done, for someone who can't feel a thing—not the table slicing through my legs when I step through it. Not the bands of rings on her fingers when I press into them.

Mrs. Gertestky's silent stare brings singes of fear to my gut, as I realize for the second time, that I might be losing everything. What if I'm even losing my ability to get others to see me? What if I'm not entirely like Wren?

I press harder. How has Wren done it all these years? Stayed in our lives, gone on living? Wandering? Being? With what has amounted to absolutely *nothing*? Nothing at all? To be in the world, but set completely apart from it?

I couldn't live like this. This isn't living—this not being able to feel the warmth from Mrs. Gertestky's skin. Not being able to hear sounds without a hollow sensation ringing in my head. Not being able to fully smell the sandalwood incense seeping from the burners on the shelves.

Mrs. Gertestky closes her eyes. "You have to want it."

I push my hand deeper into her palm, spread my fingers, then squeeze them together as if I could grab on.

She draws in a breath. "That's it. Now I can *feel* your energy. Not only see you, but feel you are there." She opens her eyes, smiles at me through a veil of sadness and pity. "It was hard enough to believe that what your friend said was true. When I first heard the story—I didn't want to believe, but now, to see you...." She shakes her head, waves an arm up. "Somehow between here and there, you are no longer with us, Myri."

"But you can get her back, right?" Roz says, leaning forward with urgency. "I mean, *she never died.*"

Mrs. Gertestky tsks. "This is hard to say. I meant what I said. The body has grown cold. It no longer recognizes Myri's spirit as its own. Very strange. I've never dealt with this. How long has this gone on?"

"A week or so," I say, not wanting to go too much into the details of my body-sharing experiences. "But it's only been a day that I've really been stuck."

She takes in a breath, rubs her hands over the circled pattern of the tablecloth. "I'm afraid our options are few, if any."

Roz gives a small cry of alarm. "Couldn't you, like, do an exorcism, or something?"

Mrs. Gertestky shakes her head. "In that, there is great risk." She takes another breath. "In exorcism, two spirits inhabit one body. In this case, there is only one spirit in one body. And one without. For Myri, exorcism could mean death."

"But Myri's right there," Roz protests. "She's still alive. Her body is alive. Her spirit is alive."

I nod vigorously in agreement. "Can't you just help me jump back in? I mean, if you forced Wren out, my body would be there for me to take back, wouldn't it?"

Mrs. Gertestky tips her head. "Maybe yes. Maybe no. Your body has adjusted to Wren in your absence. If I were to purge Wren now, there may not be a way back, not without her stepping out willingly." She looks at me, her eyes boring into mine, her fingers drum-drum-drumming the table.

"I suppose, there is one thing that may help, so we know what it is we face. We can read your future. See what destiny holds. But the question is, do you have the courage to go forward, whether one lies waiting for you, or not?"

I honestly don't know.

Am I as brave as I'll need to be?

"Yes!" Roz says, answering for me.

Mrs. Gertestky continues to wait for my answer.

Finally, I nod.

Mrs. Gertestky opens a small metal box on the bookshelf behind her, takes out three tea candles, and sets them between us. Each flame glows weakly after she lights them, swamped by their own halos of light. Giving me a nod, she covers each with an inverted tea cup. The light in the room dims.

"Choose wisely."

Chapter 37

It's late afternoon when we leave Mrs. Gertestky's shop the same way we went in—with Roz holding the door open for me before realizing she doesn't need to.

"Well, that was helpful," I say, ignoring the door as it slams shut through the back of my heels. "After all that, all Mrs. Gertestky had to say was that I'm stronger than I know."

"That's what I always tell you, too," Roz says. "Maybe now would be a good time to start believing it." She pauses, flips at a bare branch hanging low behind my shoulder. "At least the paths diverged," she adds, her voice going lower. "The smoke trails that Mrs. Gertestky said were referring to you and Wren, as tangled as they were, did eventually separate."

"Yeah, but for all we know, Wren and I could stay separated just like we are now." I swing my arms out, surprised at their weightlessness. "At least she promised to give us one night to figure this out for ourselves before she tells Mom and Gram. We've got that much."

"It's not much," Roz says, her voice flat, full of worry. She lets out a breath. "Okay, so let's start at the beginning. You've lived with Wren for fourteen years. Fourteen years without a hitch. So what's different now?"

"Going to school. Being a kid again. Learning about internal energy."

"Energy?"

"Yeah, the energy balls that Diggs has us do in drama to boost ourselves up. Wren's been into those." I stop, look at Roz, as I realize, "That is what's made her stronger. She can move things now, pick things up with her hands."

Roz's eyes go wide. "Then you've got to start doing that, too. Get your energy higher than hers."

I nod, my thoughts racing. "And Gram always says that ghosts stick around because of unfinished business."

"Well, after three hundred years, do you think Wren has figured out what that is?"

I tip my head. "She's set on kissing Duey."

Roz frowns. "We're all set on kissing Duey, but I'm beginning to think that may the downfall for us all."

I can't help but laugh. "No boy is worth this much trouble." I pause, look at the steeple of the old town church in the distance. "If we told her that it wasn't worth it, do you think she'd believe us and give my body back?"

Roz chuckles, her face going dark. "I don't know about that, but I do know *this*—you've got to get yourself back. Before tonight.

I know what it's like to be on stage. If tapping into her energy is what has made her stronger—fueled her spirit—then, if she feels the energy of finishing the play, you may never get another chance."

Chapter 38

"Roz? What are you doing here?"

If there's one person I didn't want to run into at the theater, it's my mother.

And Diggs.

But we do. Quite literally, when we round the corner at Dressing Room Two. Roz bumps into my mom, who falls back into Diggs.

Normally, this all would have been fine (even the Diggs-catching-Mom-in-his-arms-part), except that I didn't bump. I went right through them. *Both of them.*

"Oh, hi! We're looking for Wren!" Roz blurts.

My mom jerks her head in confusion. "We?"

Diggs straightens in controlled surprise, brushes the front of his blue pin-striped shirt. "Wren? Who's Wren?"

"M-Myri, I mean," Roz stammers, trying to push past them.

Mom takes a protective step toward Roz, as she looks over her shoulder. She may have been the one who said going to school would be a good experience for Wren, but apparently that idea loses its value in front of significant others. Obviously, she's not ready for these two worlds to collide.

Unfortunately, they have.

Because as she looks back at Diggs, steeling a glance past his shoulder toward the end of the hall, *I* come into focus.

"Myr—?" My mom gasps, bringing a hand to her mouth.

"It's not what you think!" I blurt.

Roz jumps to the space between us. "That's right! She's not dead!"

Diggs, realizing there are actually three people having a conversation, one of whom is not actually a full person, inches back for the wall behind him. His nostrils flare out from under his glasses in alarm.

Mom's hand flutters in front of her, as she points. "But— she's a ghost!"

"Only temporarily! She and Wren switched. *Temporarily!*"

Diggs takes in a breath, and for a moment, looks as if he might throw up. "Who's Wren?"

"*Wren's the ghost*," Roz says quickly. "Myri's not."

I wonder who's she's trying to convince more of this: them, herself, or me.

"Wren's been acting in the play. As Myri."

Mom shakes her head. Diggs rubs his forehead feverishly, looks over at me with total and complete disbelief. "I cast a ghost in the play? *In the leading role?*"

"Not intentionally. And maybe not at all, if we can get it fixed. But maybe you should prep the understudy, just in case?"

"No! Don't do that!" I blurt. "Then Wren will know that something's up. I have to surprise her."

Roz spins back to Diggs. "Okay, so Myri says hold that thought. No understudies, okay?"

"Y-yes. Yes, I heard her, as well as I can see her...."

Mom reaches for his hand, takes it in hers, searches his flustered face. Roz looks back and forth between them, gives me a wide-eyed look, and mouths, "What now?"

But there's no time to give their feelings, or mine, much thought. I give Roz a nod. "If I time it right, maybe everything will work out. But you've got to trust me."

She looks at me quizzically. "You know what you're going to do?"

"Not quite, but I will. You go find me. Keep an eye on Wren. Don't let her leave. Make sure she gets on stage."

"You're going to let her go through with the play? But Myri... her energy. It'll be affected by that. It'll grow stronger the longer she's out there!"

"I know, but it's like what you and Mrs. Gertestky have said. I have to believe I'm stronger than I know."

Roz holds my gaze, lets out a tense puff, before turning to jog away from Diggs and my mom. "Don't worry, you two. We have it under control. We'll find

Wren, and then Myri will be ready to break a leg! Just like she's supposed to."

I zip along after her, ignoring my mother's calls of my name, then her quick rush of words to Diggs that she can explain....

For a moment, I'm surprised that I'm hoping she can.

Chapter 39

"So, what do you think? Does Wren know I'm here?"

"Of course, she knows." Roz tips her head, considering. "But she hasn't acted nervous, if that's what you mean."

I've been hiding in the shadows of the curtains, making energy balls for the last hour, hoping to gain some sort of sense that I'm coming more into me—the sharpening of senses, a quickening of pulse, as if I had one. But not having experienced anything like this before, I'm not sure what I should be feeling, what might be a good sign that things inside me are starting to change.

"Have you talked to her?"

Roz is about to answer, but waits for the applause to die down at the end of the scene. "No, I've just been watching her."

She pauses as a few players brush past to get to get into position for their spots, then continues, her breath in a rush. "Look, are you sure you should be waiting this long? I mean, it's almost the end of the play. And she's practically glowing from the experience out there."

Heaviness fills my chest, as I try to nod. "I think I need to wait until I'm stronger. I pump my cupped hands in front of me. "Until I'm sure she'll be ready to let me in."

"But we're near the end of the play!"

I shrug and tell her I know, look out across the stage at Brittley, as she orders the soldiers to go to the bakery and kill Nelle, the woman with whom the prince has been spending all his time.

I'm impressed by her performance, actually. Brittley's doing exactly what Diggs said he needed her to do. Be likable as an actor, yet believable as a witch.

The lights go out briefly, as the players take up positions for the next scene. The final scene. The one where I need to get *me* back from Wren.

Before long, the soldiers are chasing her to the second story platform, calling her names. Arrows fly, and Wren falls to the floor. Duey rushes to her side.

"Here goes," I whisper, looking back at Roz. "Wish me luck."

"Wait!" She cups her hands around mine, holds them a minute. "You've got my energy with you now," she says, trying to hide her worry. "Break a leg. Or a head, or a soul, or a heart. Whatever it takes. Just make sure you come back in one piece."

I give her a quiet smile. "I will."

Then, turning to the stage, I open the door to my mind, letting all the thoughts I've been holding back of Wren rush in.

## Chapter 40

If two's company, three is definitely a crowd.

"Ewww! I should have known ye would be butting in to steal me kiss!"

Wren's voice rings in my head, as she pulls us back from Duey's lips. The kiss is over before I can even register it happened, although a few cat-calls from the audience tell me it did.

"Ye couldn't let me do it on me own, could ye, now?"

*I was hoping to not let you do it at all*, I hiss back her, my words hot my mind. *Now if it's okay with you, I'd like my body back.*

"Fine. Ye'll be getting it quicker than a cow's kick to the head," Wren replies. "Seeing that ye have ruined everything."

She's gone quicker than I expect, leaving me drowning in a thick, black void.

I try to wiggle my fingers, press weight into my elbows, get ready to sit up as Duey—I mean, Prince Bastian—declares his love a second time. But I can't get my fingers to move, or my head to lift, or my mouth to open to say my lines, and I realize that even though my eyes are closed, I can still see everything that's going on. I'm still like a ghost.

*What's wrong?* Wren asks. *Ye aren't moving yer bod.*

"Well, that's too bad." The frustration in Brittley's voice echoes in my head with a sharp intensity. "Maybe you should tell her again."

"My Lady, I said I love you!"

*Come on, Myri! What'll be holding ye back? Set into yer bod!*

I'm trying!

*Well, they're waiting. Do I need to jump back in?*

No!

Duey's face is washed in confusion.

Although I don't think he or anyone else hears me or Wren talking, it does little to calm the panic washing through me in waves. I feel too cold, too distant, too detached. I try to fill myself up with a deep-winded breath, but I can't. Not fully. It's like I'm lying in a shell that's too big.

*What on God's good earth are ye doing? Ye look like corpse posing for a picture. Go on and get up!*

I can't, Wren! I'm trying, but I can't. It's like I'm barely being held here by a mile-long thread. I can't feel anything.

*Ye must feel something, Myri, because yer energy is there. I can see it. It's there. It's red. A strong red, just like ye always are. So if it's a thread ye feel, then use that as an anchor. Grab hold and start reeling in.*

Reel it in.

*Reel it in.*

Duey looks at up at Soldier One, who is bending over him to get a better look. "She's supposed to wake up, ain't she?" he asks. "Do you think she's wanting another kiss?"

I wonder how long this scene can go on without me, how long Diggs will let them ad-lib.

Brittley stomps over my side, paces nervously. "She doesn't need another kiss! Obviously, the prince doesn't love her the way he thinks he does. His kiss didn't work, so he must still love me!"

Long time, looks like, if they go on this tangent.

"Not likely," Duey says curtly. "Unless you got the spell wrong?"

"I never get spells wrong. But...." Brittley pauses, as she looks fiercely at Duey. "But there was this *other witch* there that day when I cast the spell on Nelle. Maybe she has something to do with this. Maybe she cast a spell of her own. Maybe it's you and I that are supposed to be together."

Brittley kneels next to Duey to look down at me, letting confusion cross her face. She lets out a frustrated sigh, before lifting her eyes to his. "Kiss me, Bastian. Kiss me, instead. Don't you see? Maybe we're the ones who are meant to live happily ever after. In fact, I know we are. If it makes you feel better, we can bring Nelle with us to the castle. And if she ever wakes up, she can live there, too. She can cook and clean in the kitchen."

She leans in for kiss, whispers under her breath. "Come on, Duey, let's end it this way. Don't let her ruin the play."

I'm not going to ruin the play.

*Ye will, if ye don't get up!* Wren's voice fills my head. *Don't let her be kissing him!*

I won't! I want my life back.

*Then take it. Ye got to finish the play.*

I will.

*Good. Then ye got to be doing it.*

I'm trying! If I could just sit up, I'd take off my mask and end the play the way it's supposed to be ended.

*Ye might be wanting to do more than that, Myri.*

I do. I want to be in this world, with my mom, with my friends, even with Diggs in drama club and science class. I want to be with the people who believe in me, and show that, for once, I believe in them....

Suddenly it seems too quiet, and I realize people are waiting. Waiting for something to be done. For something to be said. And I don't know what that is. What that should be. I can't see anything.

I can't see anything....

Because my eyes are closed.

And I can't breathe....

Because I'm not breathing.

Yet, I need to....

Duey takes my hand, presses his palm against mine, sending a spark straight from my gut through my spine, making me gasp, filling my lungs with a quick rush of air.

"Forgive me, my Lady, I have failed," I hear Duey's words in my ear, his breath on my cheek. "It appears my heart belongs with another."

My eyes open to Duey's bewildered face. It's only a moment before Brittley trips back in a fluster. A camera flash sets me into momentary waves of blindness. The fleeting hope that Elise got a good photo for the yearbook does little to keep my mind from jumping into a panic, as it scrambles for a way to salvage what is left of the play.

"No, you haven't failed," I say, as Duey's eyes focus on mine.

"Myri?" He smiles with relief.

"No, Nelle."

The audience laughs.

"And you don't love another."

"I don't?"

"No. And I'll be taking that kiss."

Duey lets out a short breath, then takes in another. He gives his head half a shake, then lets a smile settle in his eyes before he brings his lips to mine.

This time, I do feel the kiss—in a warmth that shoots all the way to my belly where butterflies burst into flight.

The audience erupts into applause and whistles. When they finally settle down, Duey pulls me to my feet. "Would you be so kind to explain what just happened, my dear Nelle?"

I nod, grin. "T'was only a test that the other witch set. And you passed. *We* passed. Tell me I won't be working your kitchen?"

He laughs. "Only when you want to, and perhaps only when we want to share a biscuit with a cup of tea? As royal princess, the choice will always be yours."

With that, Duey turns to Londyn. Relief fills her face, as she jumps at the chance to finish the play. "And they all lived happily ever after."

The curtain falls, drowning out the applause. A moment later it lifts again, bringing the thunder of applause rolling back over us. My whole body tingles with excitement. I'd never imagined I'd be feeling like this on the stage.... Happy. Thrilled. Relieved. Yet, not wanting it to end.

Brittley, Cam, Cass, and the rest of the crew join hands in a line with Duey and I, as we all take our bow. And then, it's just Duey and me—the two of us, stepping forward in front of everyone.

"You were great," Duey whispers, as he pulls me off with him toward the back of the stage. "But you had me worried. You and Brittley could have told me you were rewriting the play."

"Uh... that wasn't planned. I kind of fainted."

"You did? Oh, my gosh. I didn't know.... Are you okay?"

"I am now. Lucky for us, Brittley was good enough to step in and save the scene."

"She did, didn't she?"

I let out a breath, knowing I need to thank her later. Because despite everything, she deserves it. She did help out when I least expected it. And she helped without making me look bad.

Cam calls Duey over to him at the front of the stage, and he gives my arm a squeeze before telling me he has to go. "But I'll see you afterwards? Maybe we can grab an ice cream at the mall?"

I give him a nod, tell him I think that might work, as Roz gives my other arm a squeeze.

"You, too, Roz?" he adds with a smile. "We can all go."

She tells him that would be fun.

All around me, the stage echoes with excited chatter. But there's one voice I desperately want to hear, and I'm not hearing it. A ball curls like a fist inside my throat at the thought that Wren may be gone. I dart quickly, moving among the curtains, the changing rooms, the hallways. I'm about to give up, when I suddenly see her silhouetted by a soft glow of white light near the exit door at stage-left. And she's not alone.

*C.J.*

When had he given me the sight?

The soft light grows stronger around Wren as I approach, making the knot in my throat return.

"Hey."

"Ye won't be staying mad at me now, will ye?" Wren says, giving me a worried grin.

"No, I won't be staying mad."

184

"This is Chet," she says, gesturing at the boy at her side.

"—Chet?"

"Chet Johnson," he says, extending his hand before dropping it with a foolish grin. "It's C.J., for short. You can call me C.J."

I shoot Wren a bewildered look. "The one who knew Sally Mae?"

She nods vigorously, lets out a quick laugh. "Can you believe it? He's been living at the theater almost as long as I've been living around ye home. He's not quite sure, given the bump he got on his head when, ye know,...."

"Yeah, I know." I raise my hand to Chet-slash-C.J. and give him a slight wave. "Nice to meet you."

Wren takes C.J.'s hand, making my stomach twinge with something like homesickness. "Do ye think ye can be giving us some time alone?" Wren asks him.

As C.J. moves into the shadows, a bit of light threads its way behind him.

"I'm glad ye two got a chance to be meeting," Wren says, lifting her eyes to mine.

I clear my throat, look away. It's suddenly too hard to talk, to breathe. Because I know what's happening. I've seen it a hundred times before. Only never with her.

Wren shuffles her feet.

Finally, she says, "Seeing C.J. has been so good for us both. Somehow, we both are ready to be accepting what we lost, and we're both ready to be seeing what may be left to come."

"That's great, but why go now? I mean, it's been three hundred years. What's a few more?"

Wren's face twists into a patchwork of sadness, mixed with hope and fear. "It's time, don't ye think? Ye won't be needing me."

"I don't know about that."

At first, she doesn't say anything.

Finally, I give a slight shrug.

"So, ye'll be knowing ye'll be okay, then?"

I give half a nod, as she reaches for my hand, wraps it in a tingling breeze of electricity. "I'll be missing ye," she says. "I'll be just like the sun, always chasing the moon."

"Me, too."

"Sometimes they end up catching one another, though. Don't y' be forgetting that."

"I'll be counting on it."

I manage to give her a smile.

I think I'm ready to watch her go, but when she moves toward C.J., I call her back, hold up my palm. She pauses barely a moment before holding her own up to mine.

This time, there's no chill. Only heat passes between our palms—faint, yet steady in its pulsing.

"Thanks, Wren."

"For what? I nearly left ye lying in the brink with a thousand yesterdays."

"No, you set me back on my own two feet, ready to live a thousand tomorrows."

186

"Well, I'll be feeling thankful for that, then."

"I wish I could give the same to you."

Wren smiles. "Ye have. I'll just be seeing mine in a different place."

The light fades around Wren, like a sunset being swallowed in the horizon. And then, with a flash, she's gone.

I'm alone for only an instant, before Diggs and my mother come up behind me. Diggs looks concerned, confused, but despite everything he's witnessed, appears surprisingly calm. Mom puts an arm around me, kisses a tear at the corner of my eye, then wipes a few away from her own.

"You did it, Myri," she says. "You and Wren did it. You found a way to help each other."

"I'm going to miss her, though."

Mom wraps me in her arms. "Me, too.... Me, too."

Chapter 41

Gram brings a hushing finger to her lips, shoos me off to the side of the bedroom, when I walk through the door. "We're about to witness a break-through!" she says, keeping her voice a whisper. She light-steps to the center of the room, looking back at me playfully.

Mrs. Gertestky is also there wearing her black turban, a gray paisley shawl, and white linen shirt and skirt. Her hands are cupped, held out by her side, with their palms facing upward. Her eyes, with their lids painted purple and outlined with black, are closed. And the suited ghost with the eBayed chair acknowledges her with a tip of his hat.

"What's going on?"

Gram pats the air in excitement, before taking hold of Mrs. Gertestky's hands. "We've found the train that this gentleman was waiting for when he died. The Forty-O-Seven. A steam-liner that crashed into the Potomac River before it reached his station at Harper's Ferry—can you imagine? Apparently, our client," she says, jutting her chin at the ghost, "was waiting in the station with his ticket when he suffered a heart-attack. See that stub stuck on the bottom of his shoe?" I nod, as she points at a bit of faded white paper on his heel that I hadn't noticed.

"Took a bit of head-standing to read the writing on that, I tell you." Gram chuckles, as Mrs. Gertestky gives her a knowing wink. "Anyway, we believe our ghost's wife and child were on board the train when it went off the tracks. He'd been waiting for them. He was going to join them and travel on to the Jersey Shore." She tsks at the thought, but when she lifts her eyes to mine, they sparkle with excitement. "Do you know that if this séance works, it will be a first for actually bringing back a train?"

"Here? In your bedroom?"

I look for a place to hide, saying again, "In the bedroom?" But my cry of disbelief goes unanswered, as the floorboards start to shake.

"Oo-ooh, it's working!" Gram says. She lifts her hands slightly in question. "Should we open the door?"

Mrs. Gertestky shakes her head, continues murmuring, "The doorway we need is already opened. Prepare yourself. Keep steady. Hold hands, everyone!"

Even though the corner feels safe, less exposed than the center of the bedroom, I join Mrs. Gertestsky and Gram to make a circle of three. A breeze blows through the room out of nowhere, and the blast of a train's whistle pierces the silence.

Mrs. Gertestsky pulls Gram and me over toward the bed with an iron fist. "Don't let go! Stay close!"

The walls rattle violently around us. Within seconds, the gunning silhouette of a steam engine, followed by its coal car and passenger cabins, barrels into the room, passing through the doorway and over the stairs at the end of the hall.

Wheels squeal and grind, and pipes hiss and moan, as the ghost train comes to halt in front of Gram's purchased client. With the clink of metal, the door opens before him. Pausing, he smiles for the first time in weeks up at the windows reflecting darkness back at him. After a moment, he tucks his pocket-watch inside his coat pocket, and with tip of his hat and a flip of his cane, steps aboard.

Gram mmm-hmmms with knowing delight. "Well, would you look at that." She returns his wave, which comes moments later through one of the dark panes of the passenger car. A woman holding a young child stands by his side.

As the last of three whistles stretch into silence, both the train and its passengers vanish into a brilliant flash of light.

"Well, what do you think of that?" Gram asks.

I look through the open doorway—empty and looming large. "Makes me wonder, was that the end for him? Or, another beginning?"

Both Gram and I look to Mrs. Gertestky, who considers a moment. "We all have our beginnings, Myri. We are born with them, and we die with them, too. We carry them with us wherever we go. They keep our future open and unwritten... like blank pages waiting to be filled at the beginning of a journal, or those that lie waiting at the end of a book."

Gram nods. "Endings fold over into new beginnings. They keep us moving forward, reaching out, striving to make our lives better."

I consider her words, wrap my chest up in a hug. Finally, I let out a long, contented sigh, thinking how much I like that idea.

I give Gram and Mrs. Gertestky a grin. "I know how to end this séance."

They look at each other, then back at me. "How?"

"By starting a batch of Gram's lemon cookies."

Gram laughs. "I'll race you to them. Last one to the mixing bowl welcomes the next ghost that walks through the door."

If you liked *The Ghost in Me*, there are more
stories to enjoy from the author.

Here is an excerpt from:

W
*Disasters of a T͏ₐeenage*
*Half-Vampire, Half-NOT!*

MUST – DO !!!
A.S.A.P. !!!

1. Bury the hack saw.
2. Bury the buck knife.
3. Bury all red body paint.
4. Bury the scissors, the thread—*wait, not yet.* I need these.
5. Bury latest project—not in the yard, but DEEP in the closet.

## Chapter 1. Why

It's because of the whole dead bunny thing, topped off with two rabid cats, four amputated limbs, and a dozen good-luck rabbit's-foot charms that I've taken up lying.

Okay, let's not call it LYING. Let's call it, *keeping secrets*. Out of necessity.

Because of the dead bunny.

Or, what they did to my costume. (There was actually no real bunny involved.)

Of course, I wasn't planning on the dead bunny look. I was supposed to be a cute bunny. A soft, furry, sweet one. The kind most people keep as pets.

But no. My parents had to go and change it. At the last minute. Like they always do.

Given my past experience, I suppose should have seen it coming.

Well, actually, I did. Which is why I planned for it. But then my parents went and mucked up that P.O.A., too. (That stands for Plan of Action.)

What I'd *planned* on was to hold off on the bunny costume until after the annual family photo was taken. Look like myself for the picture. After all, that's what mother does. And then, when the

194

coast was clear, I'd put the costume on, sneak out, and trick-or-treat to my heart's content.

But no. They insisted on my costume for the picture.

Until they saw it.

Then they insisted on a few improvements, i.e., cats, limbs, feet.

Which sad to say, is par for the course. The bunny was one in a long line of screw-ups.

Before the bunny, I'd suffered through being made into many other dead things on Halloween night.... There was year of the frog. That was really *quite super*—especially with the tire tracks going across my belly. And the year of the fairy (*another favorite*—they made me pluck my wings and carry them). Then, the queen—headless; and the doll—torn to shreds; and the girl—simply dead—(I gave up that year and let them paint me).

But the worst year of all was the year of the mouse. And not just any mouse. THE mouse. As in red-and-white dress, big black ears, and big, fat feet.

Yes, Minnie Mouse.

And they wound up killing her, too. It was lovely....

"Perfect," Mom said, taking a step back to admire me.

She'd painted blood around my eyes, my cheeks, my mouth.

Albert, the family skeleton, rattled his bones in agreement. "Yep, Claudette, she looks like a winner!"

"A chip off the old block!" howled Uncle Earl from his crypt.

"Nothing scarier than a dead little mouse!" cried Aunt Wilma, her voice rising shrilly with delight.

"Well, maybe a blood-sucking one," said Dad, wrapping Mom up from behind in his long, black cape. Dad was dressed as a phantom, and he was right. I, Little Miss Big Ears, looked more like a flesh-eating cannibal than a dead little mouse. It was truly terrifying, again.

But trick-or-treating was worse.

Mother went as a vampire (she's so creative), and she kept saying, "Aren't we just two peas in a pod?"

I couldn't, wouldn't, disagree. After all, it pays to be polite to a woman with fangs, even if she is your own mother.

The neighbors cringed when they opened their doors, which was what Mother wanted, of course. "What exactly are you?" they'd ask, scanning the darkness, looking for others like me.

"She's Minnie Mouse, and she's dead," Mother answered. She said this happily, matter-of-factly, as if I was one of many roaming streets that night....

But I wasn't. Thanks to the number one family rule—the one about dressing as something dead or scary on Halloween—I was one of a kind....

I'm always one of kind, simply because my idea of a happy-fun costume never passes inspection. This is why I KNOW my idea of getting dressed up in a beautiful way for Woodruff Middle School's Halloween ball will be dead in the water before I can say, "Mother, may I?"

Thus, the new plan.

The one about keeping secrets.

Since I already keep secrets on a daily basis, it may work. After all, I've had lots of practice.

You see, my mother, *Queen MV*, really *is* a vampire.

Yep, a vampire. Complete with fangs, black hair, stylish clothes....

Having a vampire for a mother is not the sort of information I can share with just anyone. If I did, there'd be things like holy water, silver bullets, and stakes-through-the-heart to worry about. Not for me—those things probably wouldn't do a thing to me. Well, I guess they would.... Silver or not, a bullet's bound to hurt....

But mix any of those things up with my mom, and it wouldn't be good. And actually, completely unnecessary, because for the most part, she's safe. I mean, she's not active. She doesn't hunt pure flesh and blood. Not entirely—she satisfies that craving with raw meat bought from the butcher.

And she doesn't sleep in a crypt like Uncle Earl. She sleeps on a California King with my dad. (He's a big guy.)

And she doesn't turn into a bat at night and fly around, but once I did see her fly out the window and catch my brother when he fell from the oak tree.

But me? Despite being born to my mother, I've never flown. Never had an inclination to hunt. And unlike my brothers, never licked a cut or scrape.

Basically, I've shown no interest in anything that turns vampires on.

Even the thought of immortality isn't appealing, because someday, someway, I do want to die, so long as it's WAY, WAY, WAY out in the future. Which for me is a long ways off. Right now, I'm thirteen.

Or, almost thirteen.

In nine months.

And I'm thinking it's about time I remind Mother.

Because thirteen is when I should be able to start doing my own thing, start making my own decisions, start taking control of my life—especially the little things.... Hmmm. Maybe I should remind Father....

After all, thirteen is when grown-ups start expecting you to act like what you're destined to be, or what you want to be, or what others think you should be when you grow up. It's an age all about... it's an age about—Eeeek!—it's an age about DESTINY!

I think I'll remind NOBODY!!!

Cripes. This business about being a vampire—or NOT being a vampire—is really going to ruin my life.

# About the Author

⇨ Shaunda is a co-author of *The Book Lover's Cookbook: Recipes Inspired by Celebrated Works of Literature and the Passages That Feature Them*. She has also written children's books, such as *In Black Bear Country*, *Caterpillar Can't Wait*, and *How Many Muffins?* for the education market. Her children's poems have appeared in *Babybug* and *Cricket* magazines. This isn't her first middle grade novel, but it came out ahead on the road to publication.

⇨ Shaunda lives in Utah, where she is perpetually entertained by her children, their friends, and the students that find themselves stuck in her science classroom.

⇨ To find out more about Shaunda and her other books, visit www.shaundawenger.blogspot.com.